AZUCAR

Moreno

AZUCAR

Moreno

SHELLEY HALIMA

A
SBI
PUBLICATION

A STREBOR BOOKS INTERNATIONAL LLC PUBLICATION
DISTRIBUTED BY SIMON & SCHUSTER, INC.

Published by

Strebor Books International LLC
P.O. Box 1370
Bowie, MD 20718
http://www.streborbooks.com

LCCN 2003116579
ISBN 13: 978-1-59309-032-6   ISBN 10: 1-59309-032-3

This book is a work of fiction. Names, characters, places and incidents are products of the author's imagination or are used fictitiously. Any resemblance to actual events or locales or persons, living or dead, is entirely coincidental.

Distributed by Simon & Schuster, Inc.
1230 Avenue of the Americas
New York, NY 10020
1-800-223-2336

Cover design: Marion Designs

First Printing December 2004
Manufactured and Printed in the United States

10 9 8 7 6 5 4 3 2 1

ACKNOWLEDGMENTS

I want to start off first by thanking the Man upstairs. Even though I've been like a wayward, hardheaded child, for some reason He's still blessed me. Thank You for answering my prayers. To my parents, Charlie and Mary, thanks for bringing me home after finding me on the side of the road (hey, Dad, I'm just going by what Mom said, smile). My brother, Dwayne—quit always cracking on me, man. I can't help it if I'm a bit weird. Also my sis, Nesey, and my nephews Marius and Chavis, I look forward to coming back to the ATL so we can finally go to the Coca-Cola Museum.

Brad Hudson, thank you for your support, your love and your encouragement—it's meant the world to me. Also, thanks for the Ernie Isley moments and the 9/1's, wink, wink. At the root of the millions of other things that you bring to my life is an awesome friendship. I greatly admire your talent and I don't know if the world is ready for a brother like you, but they'd better prepare themselves. The Living Daylights is coming!

A big thank-you has to go out to Zane. Thank you so much for believing in my work and giving me the break that I prayed so hard for. I so admire all that you're doing (and that's a LOT). You truly inspire me! I want to send thanks to the staff at Strebor, especially Charmaine Parker—thanks for working so hard for us and answering all my stupid questions, LOL! Thanks also to Destiny Wood. To the other Strebor authors (Tina, Harold, Darrien, V. Anthony, Allison, et al), I appreciate all the support and camaraderie. You all have become my second family.

Shout-outs go to the familia. Thank you to my aunts, Pat Peavy and Barbara Quinn, for all your support for my book. My cousins Timeaco (big hug for passing out the bookmarks with me), Edith and Erika. Since our family has done a bunch of procreating I'll shorten the rest to last names: The Ruckers, Danners, Quinns, Andrews, Andersons, Peavys, Edwards, and the Binns.

My partners in crime: Debra (Julius & Edward), Deanna, Barb E., Sheri, Darren, Enrique O. (aka Malcolm X), Tyronda H., Sylvia, Tony B., Robert A., James B., Bisola (we gotta hit Baker's again, girl), and Gary. Janet Brown, I can't wait for *Sing About That Black Rose* to hit the shelves. You are a caring soul who deserves all the blessings heading your way.

Got to send a hello to Reggie and the boys, Mrs. Ingram (Portia & Cortinique), Mrs. Beverly Martin and the others at Sterling Bank who took the time to read and pass around my manuscript (typos and all :-D). The Solomons (Walt, welcome to our crazy family), Dot (who's Dot?), Kathy Hudson (thanks for always making me feel so welcome), Angie Pickett-Henderson and Readincolor, TooSexyForYou, Writersrx, Tee C. Royal and RAWSISTAZ, Black Writers United, FANatic (keep on reading), Perk, Sonja (Honja), Nicole, Trevon, Mr. Romero in Colorado and Jewels Baby.

To the folks at Producto: Chris, Dawn, Bill H., Bill S., Randy G., Randy B., Charles, Danny, Rob, Chuck, Bruce, Dave, and Harvey.

Last but not least I want to send a thank-you via Heaven to Aunt Hattie. Thanks so much for all of your love, understanding and prayers. All of your words of wisdom still ring in my ears. I miss you dearly.

Shelley Halima

CHAPTER ONE / *Uno*

N oooo. Please tell me I'm dreaming about an alarm clock going off and the sound I hear isn't real. No such luck. I reach over and turn it off. I want to hibernate in bed for at least another three hours. But I can't because I have to begin preparing for the baby shower my cousin Rosie and I are throwing for our friend Rhonda. I, by the way, am Mildred Jisela Nicole Moreno. Yes, Mildred. My mother's excuse for bestowing such a name on her child is it was the first name of her former teacher, mentor, and friend who passed away two weeks prior to my birth. She wanted to pay homage to her in some way. That's very touching, but I really wish she'd planted a tree or sent a donation to the lady's favorite charity or something; if she wanted to memorialize her. Out of curiosity I asked Mami what was Mildred's middle name; thinking perhaps I could have gotten off easier. She said it was Eunice. So either way I was screwed. Needless to say, I treat that name like the proverbial pink elephant. Everyone calls me either Nik or Nikki; except for my Papi who calls me Zuzu, which is from *azucar*—Spanish for sugar.

I'm the 26-year-old product of an African-American mother and a Puerto Rican father. Some of my friends tease me and call me "blackerican." It's cool, though, because I truly feel like I've been blessed with two wonderfully rich heritages. I grew up in a world that was a wonderful mixture of soul food and Latino cuisine; Al Green and Hector Lavoe, and celebrating the legacies of Martin Luther King and Pedro Albizu Campos. I'm 5'9", 130 lbs.—that may change after all the eating I'm planning on doing today—and I have dark brown curly hair that falls right below my shoulders. I live on the West Side of Detroit. I was born in New

York, but this has been my hometown since my family moved here when I was seven. I work at a private investigation firm as an Administrative Assistant. Basically, that means I change the toner when it's low and keep track of the paper supply. It's merely a day job for me and not my career. But since I've grown attached to having a car to get around, clothes on my back and food in my stomach, I have to keep it.

The true love of my soul is acting. I'm hoping the fates decide to shine my way and one day I'll be able to survive financially from acting alone. Whenever I hear an actor say that when they first stepped on the stage they knew they'd found their calling, I know exactly what they mean. I was in my first play during my first semester of school here. I remember my teacher telling my parents after the recital how I was such a natural and they should consider sending me to a performance arts school where I could get my education, yet hone my gift at the same time. My parents ignored her suggestion.

Although they were proud of my performance, they didn't feel acting was a profession that would get me anywhere so they didn't want to encourage me. They felt, and still feel, that my acting is merely some hobby. I no longer mention any play or local commercial that I've done because, inevitably, their response is, "That's nice, but you need to put your focus on your real job at the firm."

I've never been able to make them understand that my "real job" is only a means of support and there's no way that I can envision giving up acting. People who aren't a part of the artistic world can't understand that corporate life is too confining for someone like me to be happy. I love the testing of boundaries and freeness that I find in acting. My personal hell would be being stuck in a nine-to-five for the rest of my life. I'm an artiste—darn it.

Last year my parents decided to move back to New York so it's been easier to put up with their nagging about my career choice by phone than in person. In addition to bugging me about that, they've still been pressing me for the specifics of why I broke up with my boyfriend. They really liked Jaime, but I don't want to talk about what happened with us with my parents. Jaime and I broke up about three months ago. Okay, two months, three weeks and one day to be precise.

We met in Meijer's of all places. Meijer's is one of those one-stop superstores where you can buy panties, motor oil and chicken all in the same place. I hadn't dated anyone seriously for a while and I was concentrating on my rehearsals for a play. I wasn't looking for love and I sure as hell didn't expect to find it in a store.

I was in the seafood department debating whether or not I wanted to try and cook a live lobster. Actually, it wasn't a question of whether I could cook the lobster but whether I trusted myself with getting the damn thing in the pot without dropping it or losing a finger. I was getting visions of the lobster chasing me around the kitchen, gunning for me with its cinchers. As I was standing at the lobster tank lost in thought, I heard a male voice from behind me.

"I don't know if I'd want to mess with one of those either. I'd probably go to Red Lobster."

I turned around and saw a smiling handsome face. He was about 6 feet tall, with a slim build, caramel-colored skin, a neatly trimmed moustache and a goatee. He had nice large eyes that were rimmed with thick lashes that normally take me two coats of mascara to get and he had a wonderfully engaging smile. His hair was cut close to his head—slightly faded on the sides. I'm a cologne fanatic and he had on one of my favorites—Issey Miyake.

"My indecisiveness is showing that bad, huh?" I said, smiling back at him.

"Yeah, maybe you need me to help you with your shopping because you looked kind of unsure what type of salad dressing to get a few minutes ago."

I turned and raised my hand, pretending to signal someone. "Security, I believe we have a stalker situation here."

"Okay, you got me." He shrugged innocently. "What can I say? A beautiful woman caught my eye and I had to follow her."

"Well, since you put it like that, I'll put off the restraining order for now. I've got a lot on my mind today because I definitely would've noticed a handsome man like you following me."

"My turn to say thank you. So, are you thinking of cooking lobster for a romantic dinner with your man?"

"No, for a romantic dinner with my girlfriend," I said, putting on my most serious face.

His smile slowly faded and he looked at me, as if he was not sure whether or not I was being for real. After a few seconds the quizzical look on his face made me break into a grin.

"I'm teasing you. Payback for following me around the store."

He chuckled. "You had me going for a minute there."

"For the record, I don't have a boyfriend and definitely not a girlfriend."

"That's good on both counts."

"Since you're being so nosy, wanting to know who I'm cooking lobster for, maybe you should at least tell me your name," I said teasingly as I batted my eyes, hoping to God that I didn't have any deposits in the corners of them.

"You're right," he said, extending his hand to shake mine. "I'm Jaime Darrell Dorsey. And you are?"

I shook his hand, then grinned at his playfully formal tone. "I'm Jisela Nicole Moreno. You can call me Nikki."

"Moreno? Is that Mexican?"

I shook my head. "Uh, uh, uh. You'd better be lucky you're fine or else I'd be heading to the checkout lane right about now."

"Aw, man. What I do?"

I chuckled. "For the record, my last name is Latino. Here's a quick cultural lesson. If you meet someone who is or has a name of Hispanic origin, don't automatically put them into a group such as Mexican or Puerto Rican. Just say Hispanic or Latino until you know for sure because there are Colombians, Cubans, Dominicans, Chileans, etc. That's like seeing a Native American and right off the bat calling them Cherokee when they could be Blackfoot or whatever."

"My bad. I hope I didn't offend you."

"No, you didn't. It's a bit irritating usually when people do that, but you didn't irritate me."

"'Cause I'm special?"

"Yeah, because you're special. Of course I don't know yet if it's special as in unique or special as in short yellow bus..."

"That's cold!" He leaned against the counter. "All right, beautiful lady, what's your heritage? I'm curious."

"My mom's Black and my dad's Puerto Rican."

"The mixture sure has given you an exotic beauty. You kind of remind me of that woman Vanity from Prince's old group."

"Yeah, I've gotten that before."

"And thanks for the lesson. I'll be sure to be more careful about lumping folks into a category. You'd think I'd know better as a Black man."

"Um-hmm..." I playfully pursed my lips and cut my eyes. "You're not as bad as some people. I've been asked if I 'speak Puerto Rican.'"

"Now that's bad. Do you live around here?"

"No, I live in Sherwood Forest. And you?"

"Rosedale Park, but I work not too far from here."

"Where?"

"At Office Integrators. I install office equipment, like the cubicles and built-in desks."

"My job isn't too far from here either. I work at Quinn Investigations. We do background checks and investigate insurance fraud and stuff like that." Normally I wouldn't give a guy that I'd just met any personal information, such as where I work or even the vicinity where I live. But I felt so instantly comfortable and at ease with him. No red flags were going up saying, "Possible axe murdering cannibal."

"Uh-oh. I guess you're gonna do a background check on me, huh?"

"Do I have reason to?"

"I guess I might as well fess up about my wife and six kids."

"Oh, man." I pouted. "I knew you were too good to be true."

"You know, I'm just joking with you." He grinned and we held eye contact for a minute. Oh, my stars. I didn't know if it was me or if someone had jacked up the temperature in the store.

"Wait a minute. Office Integrators...is that right off of Lilley and Ford Road?"

"Yeah, it is."

"I thought that sounded familiar. It's next to Vico Engineering, isn't it?"

"Yep, it sure is."

"I used to work at Vico about three years ago."

"For real? I've been working at OI for three and a half years. It's a small world. So there was an overlap of time when we were working right near each other. I never paid much attention over there because I'd only seen guys coming and going. You would've definitely caught my attention—like you did today. Man, that's something. So, what did you do over there?"

"I was the office assistant and the only woman in the office. I liked the guys, but let me tell you, engineers are in a class all their own. They can put the brain power on high and put together the most high-tech designs, but then will turn around and ask you how to use the pencil sharpener. 'You stick the pencil in which way?'"

He nodded. "You're right. My uncle's an engineer and even though he's smart as you know what, sometimes we wonder how he finds his way out of bed without some kind of manual."

We both expressed amusement.

"You certainly aren't doing much shopping," I said. I noticed that he only had about three items in his handheld basket. "Unless you're barely getting started."

"Nah. I was in the area and came in to get a couple of things. I can't get much in the compartment on my bike."

"You ride a motorcycle?"

"Yeah, I have a Yamaha."

"Cool! I ride a Ducati."

His jaw dropped open. "What? Are you serious? You're not playing with me again, are you?"

"No, I'm a hundred percent serious. I wouldn't lie about something that's nearly caused my parents to have simultaneous heart attacks."

"Damn! You ride?!"

"Yes. My cousin Rosie and I learned to ride about five years ago. We got our own bikes a couple of years later. We and our friend Chico go riding together whenever we get the chance."

"Man, you've earned some major points and you were already off the meter."

"Thank ya, thank ya very much."

"I won't take away points for that bad Elvis imitation."

We both chuckled.

"So, who taught you to ride?"

"My cousin's ex-boyfriend."

"You say your parents almost bought the farm together, huh?"

"Yes. My cousin and I've put some grays hairs on their heads over the years, but when they found out that we'd bought bikes, that put them over the top."

"I can imagine. My parents weren't too happy with me getting a bike, so I can see how yours would feel by you being female. They don't understand, ain't nothing like riding."

"I know. The feeling of the wind hitting you... You and I know it's a biker cliche, but feeling like you're one with the road, the freedom."

"Exactly. You might think that this sounds strange, but the only other thing that really does it for me like riding my bike is working with the earth. I love landscaping. When I was coming up, other kids used to try to get out of doing yard work but not me. The house I'm living in now, when I first moved into it, you should've seen it. The inside was nice but the yard had been really neglected. Now it looks completely different on the outside." He looked down and grinned sheepishly. "I didn't mean to go on about that. I want to make a good impression and I'm going on about my lawn."

"That's perfectly fine. I love it when people are passionate about something; no matter what it is. And you're making a very good impression, by the way."

"That's good to know. Back to the bikes. I'd like for you and I to go riding one day soon."

I blushed. "That sounds good."

"There's something about you that looks awfully familiar. It's like I've seen you somewhere. And it wasn't at Vico 'cause, like I said, I would've noticed you there."

"I act and I've done some commercials for Scarelli Leather, Solomon Chevrolet, Timeaco's Unique Boutique, Danner Soul Food, WJZZ radio station..."

"That's where! Oh, all right. So you're an actress, too?"

"Yes. My goal is to do it full time."

"What else have you done?"

"I've done some plays. Like *Soul of a Gypsy, Sasha's Song,* and the one I'm really proud of, the local production of *For Colored Girls Who've Considered Suicide When the Rainbow Is Enuf.*"

"I'm very impressed."

"And so you should be," I teased.

"You are hella interesting, Ms. Moreno. I'd like to find out more about you. How about we start by trying to tackle a couple of those together?" He nodded toward the lobster tank.

"When?"

"Tonight."

The way he said that one word and the look in his eyes...I felt a jolt hit me in the chest and travel to the southern regions of my body. We stood looking into each other's eyes for a few moments. I couldn't believe that I was actually considering packing up those lobsters and having him follow me home right then.

A grin spread across his face. "We've been formally introduced for about five minutes. I think that's long enough to make a dinner date, don't you?"

"I tell you what. Let's exchange numbers and talk before we go making dinner plans."

"That's fair."

I reached down in my purse for a pen and piece of scrap paper. I found something and began to write my number down.

"You're not giving me a bogus number, are you?" he asked with a grin that I was already in love with.

"Of course not. You'd better not really be married or anything because I'll know something is up if you try to only give me a cell or pager number."

I tore off my number and gave it to him with the rest of the paper and the pen. After he'd finished, he handed me back the paper and pen.

"There, I put my home phone, cell phone, and pager."

"I guess you can go to the lightning round now."

"Is it okay if I call you tonight?"

"It sure is. I look forward to it."

We finished doing our shopping together and talked a bit more in the parking lot before leaving. He scored points with me by not playing it cool and waiting a few days to call. He called that night, as he said he would, and we ended up talking for three and a half hours. I invited him over a couple of nights later and he brought the lobsters. I cooked them without incident. I didn't lose a finger or anything. From that night on, we spent as much time together as possible.

We were together for close to a year until it all came to an end one night about three months ago. Rosie and I had just gotten back from PR and visiting our *abuela*. After I had unpacked and settled in, I called Jaime before going to bed. We talked for a little bit, and then I told him that I was beat and going to turn in. He said that he was going to do the same. We said, "I love you," and hung up.

He called me back a few minutes later, saying that he'd forgotten to tell me that he'd received some Alexander Zonjic concert tickets from his boss. After a few minutes, we hung up again. I had dozed off into a nice slumber when I heard the phone ring yet again. I rolled over and looked at the caller ID and saw that it was Jaime. I glanced at the clock and saw that it was 12:43 a.m.; over an hour had passed since we'd talked. I picked up the phone and before I could say anything, I heard Jaime's friend Antoine talking to someone. He sounded wasted, as usual.

"Aight," said Antoine. "Don't y'all be drinkin' up my Grey Goose. That shit ain't cheap."

I wondered what Antoine was doing over there when Jaime had told me that he was going right to bed. I could hear Najee playing in the background. Then I heard two female voices, giggling and talking. I sat up in my bed, wide-awake.

"Ain't nobody tryin' to hear that," said Jaime. "You be drinking up everybody else's liquor all the time and then you wanna ration yours. Stingy ass nigga."

"Look, man, get ready to take your piece on upstairs so me and mine can have some privacy."

"Who you calling a 'piece'? I know you not callin' me a piece!" That was one of the female voices.

"Ah, baby. You know I don't mean nothing by that. So chill."

"Better not mean nothing by it."

"Is the store still open, dawg?" asked Jaime.

"Oh shit! Hello? Hello?"

I didn't say anything.

"Ain't nobody on the line, man."

"You just now realizing that? Forget it; we got enough to drink anyway."

"We'll have enough if this lush right here don't..." He hung up.

I couldn't move for a few minutes. My heart felt like it was made of lead and was beating a thousand beats a second. When I finally could will my body to move, I got up and walked across the hall to Rosie's room. I peeped through the partially open door and saw that she didn't have company and that she'd fallen asleep reading a book. I went over to her and woke her up.

"Rosie."

She was startled. "Girl, what's wrong? And there had better be something wrong, too—waking me up out of a good sleep."

"I—I..."

"What, *mi 'ja?*"

"I talked to Jaime about an hour or so ago. I told him that I was tired from the trip and going straight to bed and he said he was doing the same. Well, a few minutes ago a call came from his house. I guess his boy Antoine was trying to make a call. Jaime's got this Fisher Price phone that has a tricky redial button. A lot of times you think you're getting connected with the number that you dialed but you've actually accidentally hit the redial button. Remember when I was over Jaime's and I thought I was calling Odell and, by mistake, I ended up calling you back? Jaime kept saying he was going to get another phone..."

"Hon, you're rambling. What's going on?"

"Sorry." I took a deep breath before going on. "Okay, when Antoine called, there was smooth, cozy ass music playing in the background, I heard female voices, and Antoine told Jaime to take his 'piece' upstairs so he could be alone with his."

We were silent for a few moments. Then I saw that flint in Rosie's eyes. She tossed the book from her lap to the chair opposite the bed.

"All right, Nik. Let's put some clothes on. We're going over there. And unless there's a helluva explanation, we're gonna do some damage in the joint. You best believe that. Who does that nigga think he is?! He think he's gonna step out on you and not have to pay for it?!"

Hearing the harshness in Rosie's voice snapped me out of my stunned state and I felt the anger come over me. We both got dressed and got into Rosie's car with her at the wheel.

"Rosie, we should've brought something with us; in case those chicks wanna try and get down."

"*Mi 'ja*, I always carry at least two bats in the trunk. I'm always prepared in case some shit hits. You know that. I've got something harder than that back home; if the situation calls for it."

After a few moments of silence I hit the dashboard with my fist. "That *hijo de puta!* Damn it, I can't believe that motherfucker! How could he do this shit?"

"He's a man and shit is what they do."

"Rosie, I didn't think he was like a lot of guys out here. I thought he was..."

"You thought he was what? Different?"

"Yeah," I said softly.

"*Mira*, you'll save yourself a lot of heartache once you get past the notion that any of these *cabrons* are any different from the next. You know how many females sing that 'I thought he was different' song?"

"I wish that song wasn't on my lips right now."

"Since he put it there, we're gonna go break that nigga's head and anybody else's who gets in the way."

"As mad as I am, I don't want to hurt anybody, Rosie. Not unless somebody comes at us. I feel like smashing his windows or something."

"We're gonna send him a message, after we see for ourselves what's going on. He can't get away with doing this. All right?"

I nodded my head.

Rosie and I are more like sisters than cousins. We're only four months apart and grew up together. She's my father's niece and when Papi's new job moved us from New York to Detroit, she came with us. She's one of the few people I trust and vice versa. We've always been protective of one another. Whenever something is done to one of us, it's done to both of us. So finding out that my man was messing around on me was just like she was getting cheated on.

My cousin is straight-up gangsta, though you wouldn't know it by looking at her. All modesty aside, I'm very attractive but Rosie's downright beautiful. She looks like a Hispanic version of Cindy Crawford—mole and all. She's about two inches shorter than I am, with an olive complexion, long raven hair and a figure that would make J.Lo hate on her.

Jaime lives about fifteen minutes away but with Rosie at the wheel, we got over there in about half that time. When we arrived, we saw Antoine's beat-up red LeBaron in the driveway and a white Taurus in front of the house.

I figured the Taurus must've belonged to one of those tricks. Rosie parked next door. She popped the trunk. We got out and headed to the back of the car and each picked up an aluminum bat. We walked up to the front porch. The window to the living room was open slightly, but the horizontal blinds were closed. There were moaning sounds coming from the living room. Rosie and I looked at each other.

"Mmmm, 'Toine baby."

"I'm about to come in a minute."

Rosie pursed her lips. "Oh well, sorry, but 'Toine is gonna have to put that nut on layaway." She pushed the doorbell and knocked on the door.

I took a few steps back and looked up at Jaime's room. It was dark, except for some flickering of light. Candles. That motherfucker. I looked back down in time to see one of the horizontal blinds move.

"Oh shit!" Antoine exclaimed.

I walked to the window. "Oh shit is right! Open this goddamn door!" I shouted through the screen.

Rosie rang the doorbell again, turned around and kicked the door a few times with the heel of her shoe.

"Who the hell is that?" the female asked.

"That's Jaime's girl."

"His girl? Y'all said he didn't have a girlfriend. That's why I set him up with Tasha. I didn't come over here to get caught up in some fuckin' drama. I don't need this!"

"Shhh, keep it down, all right?"

"Don't tell me to keep it down!"

That *pendejo* Jaime had been going around telling women that he didn't have a girlfriend—having females fix him up with their friends. At that moment he was probably up in his room screwing this Tasha chick—or at least he was about to.

As Rosie continued knocking and ringing the doorbell, I stepped off the porch and loosened one of the bricks that lined the shrubbery. I stood in front of the window opposite that of the living room—the dining room. Jaime hadn't put a screen in that window yet—it was all glass. I threw the brick through the window. That bitch let out a scream; not the woman—Antoine. A few moments later we heard Jaime's voice. He was standing at the living room window pulling a blind to the side.

"Nik, what the fuck is you doin'?!"

"Open the door, Jaime!"

"You tossing bricks through my shit and you want me to let you in? What the hell's wrong wit' you?"

"I'll tell you what's wrong with me, since yo' ass is playing dumb. I know you gotta woman up in there!"

"What? What are you talking about?"

"You know what she's talking about, bitch! Now open the fuckin' door!" Rosie shouted.

Jaime pulled the blind aside farther. "Rosie. Oh, I shoulda known. You probably put her up to this, with your shit-starting ass. This is between me and Nikki and it ain't got nothing to do with you."

"Naw, nigga. If it's got to do with my cousin, then it most definitely has something to do with me! And you ain't seen no shit get started yet!"

"Look, I ain't gonna open the door so y'all can act a fool up in my house. Y'all got bats, too. Aw, hell naw!"

"So you not gonna let us in? What if we toss the bats?" I asked.

"No, I'm still not and if you don't leave, I'm calling the cops. I can't believe you busted my fuckin' window!"

No, he didn't. No, he did not. I knew that he did not say that he was going to call the *popos* on me. I looked over at Rosie and saw from the expression on her face that I hadn't misunderstood. I took one of my deep breaths.

"The reason you're not opening the door is because you have someone in there, Jaime," I said calmly.

"Nik, it's just Antoine and his girl up in here. You know his momma be trippin' if he has females over, so he brought her over here. I'm not opening the door 'cause you need to calm yo' ass down. You all outta control; throwing bricks through my window!"

"Quit being a little bitch over that fuckin' window! Now let me ask you one more time—do you have a female over visiting you?"

"No!"

"Not even Tasha?"

He didn't say anything. I heard the three of them whispering but couldn't make out what was being said.

"Uh, hello? Why you being quiet all of sudden? I said, not even Tasha?"

"Nik, I told you who's all over here."

"Negro, did I just escape from Northville? You're not even going to try and play it off and ask who Tasha is? You have somebody up in your room because you've got goddamn candles lit! And I've known you long enough to know that the only time you have candles lit is when you're fucking, or about to! Now quit trying to play me for a fool!"

"See, that's what I'm saying. You're acting all crazy. I told you I don't have anybody over and if you don't want to believe that, then that's on you. Now, for real, you and your cousin are gonna have to go. If you don't leave within the next two minutes, I'm calling the cops."

"So it comes down to this?" I felt myself choking up but I'd be damned if I was gonna cry; especially in front of him. "I'm supposed to be your woman, the one who a little over an hour ago you were saying I love you to. And now, not only won't you let me in, but you're threatening to call the cops on me? All right, I see how it is. Come on, Rosie, let's go."

"Go? Girl, we ain't going no goddamn where! Fuck him calling the cops! Shit, I've got some peeps on the force. I ain't worried. Let that muthafucka bring it!"

"Still, he ain't worth it. Come on."

Rosie outspread her arms and looked at me with a "what the fuck?" expression on her face.

"Come on, Rosie," I said firmly. I leaned toward her and whispered, "We'll be back."

As we walked off the porch I looked up at Jaime's room again. I saw the shadow of someone walking near the window. I felt my heart drop. I hate to admit it, but there was a tiny part in me that wanted to believe what Jaime had said—that it was just Antoine and his friend over. Stupid; considering what I'd heard Antoine's friend say and the two female voices I'd heard over the phone.

Rosie turned and looked in my direction. "What are you looking at?"

"Who, actually. I saw someone walk past the window."

"Girl, you sure you want to leave? We can kick down the fucking door if we have to. Or we can bust in the screen at the living room window."

"No, I've got another idea."

Once in the car, Rosie asked, "So what's up, Nik? You want to drive around a little bit and go back and surprise 'em again?"

"Not quite. We're going back home and getting some tools out the garage."

"Damn, *Mami*, what you got up? That sounds like some Mafioso shit."

"*Mira*, as angry as I am at Jaime, I'm not going to hurt him. Physically anyway."

"How then?"

"You know what Jaime loves to do?"

"You mean besides the obvious?"

"Yeah. Jaime is a fanatic about his yard. He prides himself on being this master landscaper—always talking about how he's got the best yard not only on the street, but in the whole neighborhood."

"And?"

"And we're going to fuck it up."

"Fuck up what? His yard?"

"Yes."

Rosie looked at me like I'd suggested we take a vacation in Rwanda or something. "Nikki, what kind of lightweight Teletubby shit is that?! That nigga's cheating on you. He's got some *sucia* up in his piece right now and for revenge you want to pull up his flowers?! Are you fucking kiddin' me?"

"He spends hours on that yard and practically goes ballistic if anyone even steps on the grass. Trust me, as hype as he got over me tossing that brick through his window, he'll be even more so at what we're gonna do. You're right; it is a bit lightweight. But he ain't worth the trouble we'd get into if we go with what we really want to do. At least we'll get back at him in some way, Rosie."

"I wish I knew how you can contain yourself like you do, for real. 'Cause if that was mine up in there with some bitch…" Rosie let out a sigh. "All right, we'll do it your way. So, you want to do some creative landscaping of our own?"

"You got it. Let's head back home and get what we need."

Once we got back to our house, we went to the garage. I groped and found the string and turned on the light. Rosie headed straight for a pair of electric hedge clippers and picked them up.

"Oh yeah! I can do some major damage with these, *mi 'ja!*"

I put my hands on my hips and looked at her.

"What? Why you staring at me like that?"

"Okay, Rosie. It's late and all, but why are you picking up some electric hedge clippers? First of all, we want to make as little noise as possible. And second, what are we gonna do—ring Jaime's bell and say, "Hey, we're back. Can you plug in the extension cord for these clippers so we can fuck up your bushes?'"

"Girl, I ain't even thinking. There must be some *indo* still lingering in my system."

"We're going to knock the dust off these old-fashioned clippers. Grab those two shovels over there. We'll take this rake, too. Oh, and some gloves."

"You sure that's all we'll need?"

"Yep. Let's go."

"Hey, I didn't eat on the plane and I'm starving. How about we stop and get something to eat?"

"That's cool. I haven't eaten either, and I'm going to need some fuel for our little job. Where do you want to go?"

"The only place that I can think of that's open now is White Castle. We can go get some fartburgers. Plus, we can kill a little time. I'm sure those fools have an eye out for us."

"Yeah. Hopefully, Antoine and that girl aren't still in the living room. They might hear us."

"That chick sounded pissed. I heard her say something about wanting to get out of there, so she's probably gone."

"Well, if the pussy is gone, then Antoine is gone, too."

"Antoine is the pussy. Did you hear the scream that little bitch let out when you tossed the brick through the window?"

"Uh-huh," I said with a slight chuckle. "As steamed as I was, that shit almost made me bust out laughing. Anyway, let's be out."

We put the tools in the car and ran into the house to wash our hands. Then we drove to White Castle and ordered some burgers, a sack of fries to share, and a couple of drinks. We sat in the parking lot and ate in silence. I was merely going through the motions of eating; I couldn't even taste the food. All I kept thinking in my head was, don't cry. Don't cry. Don't let the universe or anyone in it see you shed a tear over that *cabron*. Don't do it.

"You okay, girl?" Rosie asked.

"Yeah. About as well as a woman can be after finding out that her man is fucking around on her."

"See, I don't know how you're staying so calm. You should be ready to kick some ass or kill somebody."

"That's what I want to do, but I'm only going to let my anger kick in but so much."

"You certainly have gotten your temper in check over the years. You're a good one."

"No, I'm a hurt one. Part of me wants to pack it up and go home..."

"Oh, hell no! Don't even think about that shit. That mofo is gonna pay, in one way or another."

"I said a part of me wants to do that. But the bigger part wants to get back at him in some way. Oh, I'm not backing out. Believe that."

"All right. Good. Girl, you scared me for a minute." She looked at me for a second. "But just in case that other part starts taking over, let's get on over there so we can get some type of revenge on him; even if we only pull up some damn tulips."

Rosie gathered up our containers from the food, got out the car, and took it all to a nearby garbage bin. She climbed back in and started the car. "You ready, cuz?"

"I'm ready."

We drove back to Jaime's house. By then, Antoine's car, as well as the white Taurus, were gone. Rosie parked about two houses down. We got out with everything and went to work. The street and porch light helped us to see a little. We loosened the bricks surrounding the bushes near the porch and placed them quietly on the porch. I raked all the red-colored chips that surrounded the shrub onto the grass. We hacked away at the shrubbery; then the flowers, pulling out the roots. We dug holes in the lawn with the shovels—hurling some of the dirt and grass onto the porch. Luckily, it had rained earlier, which softened the ground, making that portion of the job much easier. By the time we were done, we were two sweaty pieces of funk. We tiptoed to the sidewalk, maneuvering around the holes. We stared at our work, then looked at each other and grinned.

Rosie leaned over toward me and then sniffed. "Whew! You are ripe."

"You ain't exactly a fresh flower in spring yourself, heifer. Let me do one more thing and we can leave."

I walked around to the side of the house and got the water hose. I brought it around to the front and placed it in one of the holes near the middle of the lawn–or what was left of it. I went back and turned on the water full blast.

"Let's go," I said as I came back to the front.

We gathered the tools, put them in the trunk and left. As soon as we got home we went to our bathrooms and took showers. It was weird but, as I was taking my shower, I felt like I wasn't only cleansing my body of dirt and sweat, but of Jaime as well. I felt a bit numb, with little spurts of hurt peeking through, threatening my tear ducts. It was going to take a minute, but I was determined to get over it. To me, infidelity was the ultimate betrayal and I knew that I'd never feel the same way about Jaime.

Still, I did—do love him. Sooner or later those tears I was holding in were going to come full force. I kind of wished that I'd taken the high road, but fuck that. He deserved what we did that night. Shit, fucking up his pride and joy was nothing compared to what he'd done to me.

That morning, the sound of the phone ringing jolted me out of my sleep. I saw from the caller ID that it was Jaime. My first inclination was to ignore the call, but then I decided I might as well get the shit over with. I reached over and picked up the receiver.

"What?"

"Don't *what* me, goddamnit! What the fuck's wrong wit' you? You and your crazy ass cousin fucked up my shit!"

I had to pull the phone away from my ear because he was screaming so loud.

"Look, you need to relax yourself."

"Relax myself? Relax myself? You know damn motherfuckin' well how much time and money I put into my yard! I ought to file a police report and then sue both you psycho bitches!"

"You better watch it with the bitch shit. 'Cause if anybody is a bitch, it's you. Your bitch ass wouldn't even open the door last night." My voice sounded calm and controlled to my ears, but anger was simmering right beneath the surface.

"What the fuck I'ma open the door for when y'all acting all off the chain—throwing shit through my window and standing on the porch with bats?"

I shook my head. "You're still sticking to your story that you didn't have a woman over, aren't you?"

"It ain't no story. That's merely your jealousy and your cousin messin' wit' your head. I told you that it was only Antoine and his female friend over. Goddamn it, I didn't call you to talk about that bullshit! I'm calling to talk about how you..."

"So, if it was only you, Antoine, and his friend over, who was that walking around in your bedroom?"

"What?"

"You heard me. While you three were downstairs, someone was walking around in your room. I saw their shadow by your window."

"We-wha—, I don't know what you thought you saw..."

"Motherfucker, stop trying to play me for a fool!" My simmering anger rolled into full boil. "You know you had a bitch over there, so quit insulting my fucking intelligence! Be a man and own up to yours!"

There was silence on the phone.

"All I have to say to you, Jaime, is number one—fuck you! Number two—you're a lying, cheating, no-good ass bastard. Number three—messing with your stupid yard was the least I could've done. Because if I had let my emotions take over, I would've burned your ass out of that house! And one last thing—fuck you!" I slammed down the phone.

About a week after that, the masochist in me made me drive by his house one night. Parked in his driveway was the white Taurus. There were no lights on in the house. I knew she was there, in his bed—this faceless Tasha. I wondered if they were sleeping the way we used to, naked and on their sides with him behind her, his arm draped across her waist, his face nuzzling her neck. Was he waking her up in the middle of the night to make love again? I drove around a bit until I had to pull over because of my blurred vision from the tears that I finally couldn't hold in anymore. I must've cried for half an hour straight.

Right now I'm getting through the stages that follow a bad breakup. I've gone through the "I want to filet his dick and saute his balls" anger stage. And the "oh God, why does it hurt so bad, how could he do this to me?" crying stage. It's happening a lot sooner than I thought it would, but I'm moving into the "Jaime died? That's too bad—what's for lunch?" apathy stage.

I guess I'd better roll my ass out of this bed. I'm glad we did the housecleaning and some of the cooking last night, because that's less to do today. By *we* I mean Rosie, our friend Chico and me. We share this home, a brick Colonial that I inherited from my maternal grandparents. They died two years ago in a car accident on their way back home from a weekend spent on Mackinac Island.

I love this house. I always have. However, I hate the means by which it became mine. Rosie and I spent many summer vacations in PR but most holidays and weekends were spent here after we moved from New York. Coming over here is what helped make the transition of the move go much more smoothly. My grandparents were very lively, affectionate people who loved kids. We had more toys here than at home. They always came up with interesting things for us to do. I don't believe that either Rosie or I ever uttered, "We're bored, there's nothing to do." They'd mastered the art of spoiling us monstrously without turning us into spoiled monsters.

As soon as I make the move to get out of bed and head to the shower, I realize that I'm horny as hell. I've been going crazy lately. I haven't had any *pinga* in over three months now. It's been hard adjusting from getting it on the regular to *nada*.

Time to pull out my old friend from the nightstand. I got this little gadget from a sex toy party that Rosie hosted. I call it Hector. This thing can make a repressed Mormon—that was redundant—explode in less than five minutes. You insert the phallic-shaped part inside of you, and attached to the base is this animal, a beaver—appropriately enough, with its tongue sticking out. That rests on your clit. When you turn it on to vibrate—woo hoo!

My trip to bliss only takes about three minutes. Whoever invented this vibrator needs to win a damn Nobel Peace Prize or something. If I knew their name I'd add them to my Christmas card list. It's the least I could do.

CHAPTER TWO / *Dos*

As soon as I'm dressed I go and wake up Rosie. I walk across the hall and tap on her door a couple of times. I get no answer so I turn the handle, find that it isn't locked as usual, and peek in.

Well, well, well. Someone's getting laid around here. In the bed with Rosie is some chick. All I see is a mass of long black hair covering her face. I tiptoe to Rosie's side of the bed.

"Rosie," I whisper as I lightly shake her.

"Huh?"

"Wake up, girl."

"What?"

"We gotta get cracking, *mi 'ja.*"

"Aw shit."

"I know, I know. I didn't want to get up either, but we've got a lot of cooking to do. Plus we gotta put up the balloons and banners. Oh shit! I forgot we have to pick up the cake!"

"What time is it?"

"Nine-fifteen."

"All right, Mami, I'll get up in a minute. I've got to take Lori home and I'll stop by the bakery on the way back."

"*Chevere.* I'm going to get cracking on the food."

"Okay."

Rosie turns back to Lori, kisses her on the shoulder, and nudges her to awaken her. I take that as my cue to make a swift exit and head downstairs to the kitchen.

Rosie and I never lacked attention from the boys at school and in the neighborhood. And I'm not going to front, we loved it. On her 18th birthday, after a couple of Sea Breezes and some Jell-O shots, she confided to me that though she liked boys, she liked girls as well. I'd be lying if I said I was shocked. I had for a while suspected that something was going on between Rosie and her friend Toya. Once I'd walked in on them hugging. They'd explained that Rosie was only comforting Toya because she and her boyfriend had broken up. I didn't buy that, but pretended that I did. The hug I'd witnessed was too intimate to be that of simply a friend comforting another. After that incident, I'd observed more. Like the little furtive looks and touches they exchanged when they thought I wasn't paying attention. I never said anything. I knew Rosie would tell me what I was suspecting in her own time. When Rosie came out to me that night, she confirmed that she and Toya were indeed lovers.

Shortly thereafter, Rosie became comfortable with her sexuality and was more open about it. When word got back to Papi, he wasn't pleased, to say the least, and wanted me to move out of the apartment that Rosie and I were sharing at the time and come back home. Though he loves Rosie like a daughter, in his old-fashioned way of thinking, he was scared her lifestyle would rub off on me. I stood my ground with him and assured him that he had absolutely no cause for concern in that department. Rosie's coming out helped me out in one area. After Papi found out about Rosie, he didn't give me any more lectures about my boyfriend spending the night. He was thankful that I was into men only.

Our circle of friends, though surprised when they found out, were supportive of Rosie. There were some members of our family back in NYC who weren't as accepting, but Rosie couldn't care less. She said the only person in the family she was worried about was me and I told her that she could be getting it on with transgendered gargoyles and I wouldn't love her any less. Of course, in that instance, I wouldn't drink behind her.

As I head downstairs, I stop at the bottom of the stairs in the small foyer. There is a coat rack and a cherrywood table. On top of the table is a vase of fresh flowers—orchids. My grandmother always had fresh flowers right here in the foyer, if nowhere else. She wanted guests to be greeted by their fresh scent as they entered the home. That's a tradition that I keep alive for her. Hanging above the table is a black and white framed picture of one of my grandfather's and my favorite musicians—John Coltrane. The picture is a bit askew so I straighten it. The flooring is a tan and cream-colored marble that my grandfather put in himself.

To the left of the foyer is the living room. It's decorated in a mixture of burgundy, camel, and deep browns. There are two plush sofas facing each other and directly in front of them, taking up almost the entire wall is an oak entertainment center that houses a television and stereo system. To the side of that is a 50-gallon aquarium that practically illuminates the entire room when the light is on. It has many exotic fish that were not cheap, but the tranquil quality it adds to the room makes it well worth the price.

Leading straight from the living room is the dining room. It has a large table that seats eight, a matching buffet table and, to the right on the opposite wall, is a china cabinet. My grandmother kept it in excellent condition by cleaning it at least twice a week. Of course, I make sure to do the same. Since this home was already furnished so beautifully, Rosie and I gave away the furniture we had when we moved in here. My grandparents had really excellent taste and somehow our secondhand IKEA furniture wouldn't have quite worked in here anyway.

My favorite room in the entire house is the kitchen. This was, and still is, the epicenter of the home where everyone congregates. It's a nice-sized kitchen with an island in the middle. The stove and the oven are separate and built-in; the stove into the counter and the oven inside an opposite wall. Grandmother had planned to have a fireplace installed near the breakfast nook, but she didn't get the chance. She decorated the kitchen in a nice homely-style, with sort of a country—but not too country—flair.

I think I'll make an omelet or something before I start cooking, because if I cook on an empty stomach, I'll eat up everything as quickly as I make it. As I reach into the fridge for the eggs and milk, I hear someone walking up the basement steps into the kitchen. I turn and see Chico bringing up a basket of clothes.

"Morning, sunshine."

"*Buenos dias.* I'm about to make an omelet. You want one?"

"Shoot, hungry as I am, I'll have three."

"One omelet coming up."

"Smart ass." He sets the basket on the floor next to the wall. "You know some sausage links sure would go good with those omelets."

"Give you an inch... Get them out of the refrigerator."

"Thanks."

"Uh-huh."

Chico is my boy. I love his baldheaded ass to death. Not in a romantic way, but in a the-brother-I-never-had way. He's a really cute guy, about 5'10", light-skinned with hazel eyes. He has a slightly husky build but the weight looks good on him. His real name is John Esposito. I gave him the nickname Chico when I noticed how much he looked like R&B singer Chico DeBarge. It's funny because, back in the day, Chico had long curly hair, just like the singer used to. Then our Chico shaved his head bald. Right after that Chico DeBarge came out of jail and back on the music scene—baldheaded, too.

Like me, Chico's mixed. His mother's African-American like mine, but his father's Italian-American. As soon as we moved to the neighborhood, he and his brother, Mario, who is two years younger, made it their mission to pick on Rosie and me. They did regular boy stuff like spraying us with their water guns, sneaking up behind us and yanking our ponytails, scaring us with bugs, etc.

Rosie and I let them slide for a while because we thought they were cute. They were jerks, but they were cute jerks. Then one day we were walking down the street on our way to play at a new friend's house. It had stopped raining after a two-day downpour and the ground was soggy wet. We were jumping over puddles every few steps. We had gotten as far as Miss Delia's house. Her five kids played on the lawn so much till it was nothing but a dirt field with a few stubborn blades of grass poking through. After the rain, the lawn—as it were—was a virtual mud bath waiting to be taken.

Creeping up behind us, Chico pushed me hard from the side into Rosie and we both fell into the mud. He ran off down the street. He stopped for a moment a few doors down and looked back at us, bent over with his hands on his knees, and cracked up with amusement. We were wearing brand-new, matching, pink short sets and white socks and gym shoes that were now mud-soaked. That was it. Throwing us in the mud was bad enough. But to throw us in the mud in our cute new outfits was an unforgivable offense that called for retaliation; cute boy or not. Rosie and I decided we were going to look for an opportunity to do a sneak attack of our own. Our time came three days later when we saw Chico riding his bike into his backyard. We'd seen Mario leave for Little League practice earlier so we knew he wouldn't be around to help Chico.

We tiptoed into the backyard and saw Chico squatting down next to his bike, pumping air into one of the tires. His back was to us. Rosie pushed him to the ground and we both went in for the kill. We beat the crap out of him. He only managed to get in a hit here and there. I don't know if it was Rosie's blow or mine, but he ended up with a bloody nose.

After that his attitude changed toward us. He didn't pick on us anymore and actually intervened when Mario tried to. I couldn't figure out if it was because he had gained a newfound respect for us or if it was because he was scared that we'd tell everybody that two girls beat him down. In any case, by the time we got to middle school, we were really tight; Mario included.

"Hey, what time did you say Mario's plane gets in?"

"Three-fifteen. Oh, by the way, I gotta couple of my boys from work coming also. Is that cool?"

"Ain't no choice but for it to be cool. You've already invited them. No, seriously, the more the merrier."

"Man, they looked at me like I was crazy when I first invited them. They were all like 'a baby shower'? I had to let them know that it's different from the ones they're used to hearing about."

Some people, well most people, would find it strange that guys are even interested in coming to a baby shower. But this isn't a traditional baby shower. The Puerto Rican version of a baby shower is basically a party. It's not only for women, but for men and children also; though we specified that the only kid invited to this one is the one in the mother's belly. That's so us adults can feel free to be adults without impressionable eyes all about. There's going to be lots of food, drinks, music and gifts.

"I see, or rather heard, Rosie had some company over last night. She was going at it most of the night. You're lucky your room is across the hall. My room's right next to hers and, trust me, the girl is vocal."

"Gee, Chico. Sure ya not jealous?" I ask, smiling.

"Shit yeah. That girl gets more pussy than I do. She plays for both teams, but it seems like she's only been playing for one side lately."

"No, she still sees Alejandro from time to time. He's in love with that girl. He's hasn't been coming over as much 'cause he's hurt by the fact she's not giving him a real chance. She cares about him also but she's resisting it. I think it's because she's letting this torch that she's been carrying for someone else get in the way. I told her that she shouldn't let that interfere with what she could have with Alejandro, since she knows that she doesn't have a chance with this other person."

"Who is this other person? Anybody I know?"

"I could tell but then I'd have to kill you."

"Oh, it's like that?"

"Yeah, it's like that."

"All right, keep your secrets then." He takes a sip of orange juice. "I'm glad Mario finally got some time to come here. It's been rough not seeing my little bro that often since he moved out to L.A."

"Yeah, I'll be glad to see that knucklehead. I can't wait to have some of those famous margaritas of his."

"Me, too. So what all are we having to eat at this shindig?"

"Everything for everybody. Buffalo wings, potato skins, *tostones*, ceviche, shrimp *mofongo*, *chuletas de puerco*, *pastelillos*, potato salad, Odell's bringing some banana pudding, and Crystal's mother's boyfriend is cooking some ribs. Plus, other people are bringing dishes like greens and stuff."

"Mmmm. I'll be at the gym first thing Monday morning."

"I'll be right beside you."

Chico and I finish our breakfast and he washes the dishes. I glance at the clock. Just then Rosie enters the kitchen.

"It's about time," I say. I peek around and see that Lori isn't walking behind her. "What were y'all doing, still bumping beavers?"

Chico shakes his head.

"Well, since you gotta be all up in mine, yes, I had to get me a little quickie in."

"Oh, brother. Where is she?"

"She'll be down in a minute."

"I was telling Nikki that you need to get your room soundproofed or something, with your loud ass."

"Aw, boo, you jealous?"

"That's what I said," I tell Rosie.

"Chico, I promise if you're a good boy, I'll invite you to join in one night."

"Yeah right. Promises, promises. But I'd be a happy man if you did. Let me know and I'll bring my jimmies, a camera, and my eight inches."

Rosie and I snicker.

"That's all you got, *nucca*, is eight inches?" asks Rosie. "Shoot, I got ten inches."

"What?" Chico says. "What the heck you talking about?"

"My strap-on. I got a nice big black one."

"Aww!" Chico and I say in unison, throwing up our hands.

"TMI, Rosie. Too much information."

"Chico, don't hate 'cause what you got doesn't vibrate and rotate like mine does," Rosie says as she pokes him in the side with her finger.

Chico tugs at his crotch. "Ain't nothin' like the real thing, baby. That's all I got to say."

"I know that's right," I say.

"You got one of those things, for real?" Chico asks.

"Heck yeah. And I've had some very satisfied lovers, too," she says, moving her neck from side to side.

Chico looks at Rosie, his face scrunched up.

"What's wrong with you?" she asks.

"That ain't a good picture you've put in my head. Now when I look at you, I'm going to have the image of your yellow ass with a big black plastic dick strapped on."

"Eww!" I say.

We all cackle.

Rosie grabs an apple off the counter.

"Look, Rosie," says Chico. "Uh, not to bring the room down but your mom called again last night. She really wants you to call her."

Rosie's face instantly hardens.

"She really wants me to call her, huh? Oh well, people in hell really want Popsicles but it don't mean the Good Humor man is gonna be rolling through, now does it?"

"What did she say, Chico?" I ask.

"Who the fuck cares what she said, Nik?!" Rosie asks hotly. "I don't. And if you're down with me like you're supposed to be, then you shouldn't care either!"

"Don't get hype with me, Rosie. You know I'm down with you. Don't ever fix your mouth to say some shit like that again. I'm just asking, in case it's something important this time."

"There's nothing important that she has to say to me. 'Cause I don't have a damn thing to say to her. I don't give a fuck about her and I ain't trying to hear anything that comes out of her mouth!"

I stand there with my arms folded, looking at her. Her face is flushed to a deep red. She gets upset talking about her mother. Through all the cuss words, she's still hurt from what went down with her mother. No one gets that upset over someone they "don't give a fuck" about. At that moment, Rosie's friend is walking toward the kitchen. She looks like she's either a dark Asian or is Asian and black. She's petite and really pretty. Her long black hair is pulled up into a ponytail. She walks over to Rosie. She smiles shyly at Chico and me. Rosie puts an arm around her waist.

"Hi," Lori says softly.

"How you doing?" asks Chico, smiling from ear to ear.

"Hello," I say.

"Lori," Rosie says. "This is my cousin Nikki and our friend Chico. Everybody, this is Lori."

"Nice to meet you," Chico and I say together.

"Same here," says Lori.

"Sorry to make this intro so short, but I gotta take Lori home so she can get ready for work and so I can get back here. I should be back in about half an hour or so." Rosie looks at me and comes over and pretends to take a jab at my cheek with her fist. That's her way of apologizing for raising her voice to me. "See ya, Nikster."

"See ya, heifer."

"Bye," says Lori.

Chico and I both say, "Bye." Rosie takes Lori's hand and they head down the steps to the back door.

"Drive carefully, Maria Andretti," I call after Rosie.

"*Si, madre, si.*"

Once they're out of the house, Chico turns to me. "Damn, that girl is fine! How Rosie be pulling honies like that? I need to roll with her!"

"All right, calm down before you have to change your pants."

"Did you see her breasts?"

"No, fool! I wasn't checking out her chest."

"They were like two perfect melons. I'm pretty sure they were real. They moved like they were. You know, with that bit of a jiggle? Fake breasts don't move at all."

"Boy, I ain't even trying to sit up and talk about some chick's melons, as you call them. I'm only concerned about my own melons, thank you very much."

"Yeah, you do have some nice ones." He reaches out like he's going to touch them.

I giggle and slap his hands away. "Do you have everything ready for Mario downstairs, idiot?"

"Yeah, I changed the sheets on the sofa bed and vacuumed. It's nice as hell. It's like a little apartment. I think after he leaves, I'll move down there. I don't know why I didn't do that in the first place."

"You should. Then you won't be subjected to all of Rosie's sounds of passions."

"True dat. Let me take these clothes upstairs."

When Chico leaves, I start preparing the food. As I do so, I think about Rosie's response to her mother's phone call. I do understand her decision not to have anything to do with her mother. But I still wish that somehow they could get past everything and have some kind of decent mother/daughter relationship. I won't hold my breath though.

The beginning of the end of their relationship took place back in New York—months before our move to Detroit. My parents and I lived in an apartment a few blocks away from the one Rosie shared with her mother, Lupe; her brother, Raul; and her stepfather, Renaldo. Tia Lupe had recently remarried. She had done so almost exactly six months from when her husband and my dad's brother, Guillermo, had died of a brain aneurysm. Renaldo was their downstairs neighbor and had also been Tio Guillermo's poker buddy. I heard Tia Lupe telling Mami that she was getting remarried so soon because she had never worked and she had no job skills, and she needed a husband to look after her and her children.

Neither Rosie nor I cared for Renaldo. He gave us the creeps; so much so that when he would give us treats, we wouldn't even eat them. He was tall and had a slender build. He was a decent-looking guy; except for the long scar on his face. It ran from his left ear, along his cheek, ending near the left side of his mouth. Even more menacing than the scar were his eyes. They were dark, almost black. They were not only dark in color but they felt black. If someone were to ask what I thought a monster's eyes looked like, I would've chosen Renaldo's as the point of reference. The fact that his breath smelled like shit didn't exactly help him to win any brownie points either. Rosie and I thought that if Tia Lupe had to remarry so soon that it would've been to Renaldo's brother Tony instead. He was much nicer and took the time to play with us; as if he really wanted to. Not like Renaldo, who seemed to only take an interest in us when another adult was around. It was like he was trying to show off that he liked kids or something.

As soon as he and Tia Lupe married, he practically shut out the family. We'd drop by for a visit and knew that they were home, but no one would come to the door. I wasn't welcome to come over after school anymore or to sleepover. I overheard my parents talking and Papi was fuming, saying it was like Renaldo was keeping them prisoner in that apartment. Renaldo even pulled Rosie and Raul out of St. Mary's and enrolled them in public school.

One day, after a few weeks of having not seen them, Mami and I ran into Rosie and Tia Lupe at the market. Mami and I rushed over to greet them. Tia Lupe seemed nervous and frazzled and Rosie looked miserable. Mami pulled Tia Lupe over to the side and they spoke in hushed tones. I stood there looking at Rosie as she stared down at the floor. I knew something was wrong, terribly wrong, with my cousin. I couldn't even find the words to ask her; maybe because I was afraid of what the answer would be. I reached out and held Rosie's hand and it rested limply in mine.

Shortly, Tia Lupe came back over and said to Rosie that they had to leave. Mami pleaded with Tia Lupe to please call the family; everyone was worried about her and the kids. I released Rosie's hand and hugged her. At first she didn't hug me back, then she hugged me—tightly. I felt Tia Lupe pulling on Rosie's coat, telling her to come on.

We finally let each other go and when we did, I saw a tear roll down Rosie's cheek. I knew she couldn't tell me right then what was wrong. I brushed away the tear with my mitten-covered hand. She and Tia Lupe then went to the checkout lane. I went and stood near the lane they were in, staring at Rosie. She turned around and looked back at me. It was like we were trying to communicate with each other, in some unspoken way. Mami told me to come with her and finish shopping. I refused to move. She gave in and told me to find her in the store when I was ready. My eyes never left Rosie until she and Tia Lupe left the store.

A week later, after everyone was in bed, we were awakened by the sound of someone furiously ringing the buzzer. I sat up in bed. I saw Papi walk hurriedly past my room to the living room to see who it was. Moments later, I heard him say, "Rosie, what's wrong?" I jumped up immediately.

When I got to the living room, I saw Papi kneeling down near the open door, holding Rosie, who was crying uncontrollably. She was wearing only her night-gown and house slippers. Mami came into the room and stood behind me with her hands on my shoulders. We both stood still, transfixed, dreading to find out what had brought Rosie to our home in such a state. Papi closed the door, picked up Rosie and carried her to the couch. I finally found the will to move. I went and sat next to her and held her hand—it was ice cold. She was shivering. She had run from home in the February night air. Mami brought out a blanket and wrapped her up in it.

Papi asked her what had happened. Mami said that I should go back to bed. Rosie adamantly said, "No!" She wanted me there. Papi asked her again to tell us what was wrong but she wouldn't say. After some gentle prodding from Mami, Rosie said that she'd tell, but only to Mami and me. There was a stricken look that washed across Papi's face, like he already knew what was wrong. Papi got up and kissed Rosie on the forehead and then left the room.

After some minutes had passed, Rosie was ready to tell us what happened. She said that he'd been messing with her in a bad way—touching her down there and he'd made her touch and kiss his "privacy." That night he'd come into her room. He'd taken off her panties and tried to put his thing inside her. She said that it hurt really badly. She'd pretended that she had to go pee and begged him to let her use the bathroom. He did and she sneaked out of the apartment and ran.

Mami asked her where her mother was when Renaldo was doing this. Rosie looked at Mami and said it wasn't Renaldo who'd been messing with her. It was his brother Tony. I was shocked. I'd assumed, like Mami, that it had been Renaldo. I'd liked Tony, until that moment. I'd thought that he was nice, much nicer than his brother. Tia Lupe and Renaldo were at the hospital with Raul, who'd had another asthma attack. Tony had come over to watch Rosie.

She said that she hadn't told anyone before about Tony touching her the other times when he was alone with her because he said everyone would call her a bad girl and no one would love her anymore. Mami hugged Rosie and assured her that she wasn't bad at all and that no one was going to stop loving her. Rosie stared at me, as if to confirm this. I grinned and nodded my head in agreement. Mami took Rosie into the bathroom to give her a bath. She came into my room to get a pair of my underwear and one of my nightshirts for Rosie.

We knew Mami had told Papi because later, when Rosie and I were lying in bed, we heard him pound the wall, cursing in Spanish and English. He said that he was going to kill that son-of-a-bitch. We heard Mami trying to calm him down. Rosie and I clung to each other. I wanted all of it to be over so that we could get back to jumping rope and playing jacks. Rosie started telling me about the situation at her house since Tia Lupe had married Renaldo.

He treated her and her mother like crap—always shouting at them and saying that they never did anything right. Every day before he left for work he'd give her mother a list of things to do and a schedule of the times they were to be done. Even though he wasn't there, Tia Lupe would follow the schedule to the letter; despite the fact that she did those things on her own anyway. Raul was spared all of this. He was the son Renaldo never had but always wanted. Raul had always been a bit of a brat and now he took full advantage of his favored status in the house. He'd make Rosie do his homework and tell every little thing she did.

Later, just as we'd drifted off to sleep, we heard the phone ring and then Papi saying loudly that Rosie wasn't missing, she was there, was going to stay there, and that he was coming over their place first thing in the morning. We knew he was talking to Renaldo or Tia Lupe.

The next morning, Mami and Papi said that we were staying home from school and that they were going over to Tia Lupe's. Papi said they'd be back soon and to be sure not to let anyone in. They returned a few hours later with suitcases and garbage bags filled with Rosie's clothes, toys, and books. Papi told Rosie that she'd be staying with us. Rosie didn't say anything, but nodded her head.

We were both happy that she wouldn't have to go back and would be living with us, but we were curious as to what had taken place when Papi and Mami had gone over to Tia's. I asked Mami, but she said that was grown folks' business. Parents should realize that, hard as they may try to, they can't keep much from kids. Children's ears are always open and ready to receive information. So of course we found out what had happened a couple of days later. Rosie and I were in the bedroom. We'd just finished eating peanut butter and jelly sandwiches and drinking Kool-Aid and were brushing the hair on our dolls.

I was telling her about how the kids at school were saying that Sister Gloria was really an evil witch in disguise. Joey Ramos swore he saw her floating down the hall—the bottom of her habit was at least four inches off the ground. Juanita said that the burn mark on Sister Gloria's face was probably from when someone sprinkled her with blessed water. All of a sudden, Rosie shushed me. She went to the door that was slightly cracked and opened it a little more. I put down my doll and followed behind her. We heard Papi on the phone. We caught that he was speaking to our *abuela*. He was saying that Rosie was staying with us. He said he was furious with Lupe and that Guillermo was probably turning in his grave. He'd told her and Renaldo what Tony had been doing to Rosie. Renaldo said that Rosie was lying and Tia Lupe went along with him.

Papi told them that no child would run out into the cold winter night with only a nightgown and slippers on without a damn good reason. And that when Mami had examined Rosie in the bathroom, she saw that Rosie had bleeding down there. Papi wanted Tia Lupe to file charges against Tony. Renaldo told Tia Lupe that if she did so he would leave her on the spot and have their marriage annulled. Papi told them that if they weren't going to go to the police, then Rosie sure as hell wasn't going to come back to that house and she'd stay with us instead and, if they didn't agree, then he'd go to the police himself. Tia Lupe gave in and agreed that Rosie could come live with us. Papi said something about having Rosie see a counselor. Rosie closed the door and we both went and sat on the bed.

I felt tears stinging my eyes. How could Tia Lupe not stand by Rosie? Why would she say Rosie was lying about something like that? Why would she choose to stay with that scarred-up monster instead of being with her daughter? I looked over at Rosie, expecting to see her crying as well. Instead her face was set and hard. After a few moments she said that she'd never forgive her mother and she never wanted to see her again. She threw her doll against the wall.

Despite what she said, I often saw the hopeful look Rosie got sometimes at the sound of the phone ringing or someone buzzing the door. She was expecting her mother to come and say that she'd left Renaldo and for Rosie to come home. I was expecting the same thing. I loved having Rosie living with us, but she wanted to be with her mother. It never happened. Tia Lupe would only sporadically call and see how Rosie was doing. We heard through the family grapevine that she had to sneak and do that because Renaldo had forbade her to even contact Rosie at all. Most kids will overlook the shortcomings of their mothers; no matter what they do. But Rosie took her mother's actions into her soul and the anger over it has only festered over time.

A few years ago, we found out that Renaldo had left Tia Lupe for another woman. Lo and behold, a short time later she got Rosie's number and called her, trying to reconcile. Rosie told her mother not to call her anymore. She'd made her choice and she was going to have to live with it, since she wanted to be some-one's wife more than she wanted to be her mother. Tia Lupe tried to explain that she was so afraid of Renaldo and that's why she'd done what she did. Rosie wasn't trying to hear it, and still isn't. Tia Lupe gave up for a while, but recently she's been trying again.

Even though Rosie lost contact with Raul for many years, he got in touch with Rosie a few months ago. He told her that it'd be great if somehow she could have a relationship with their mother, but he understood how Rosie felt and wouldn't hold it against her if she didn't. His main concern was getting to know his sister again. When he was younger, Renaldo had convinced him that Rosie was a trouble-maker and said that she was no longer a part of their family. Once he got older, he saw things for how they really were and resented all the time they'd lost together. He said he would've called sooner, but he didn't know whether or not Rosie wanted to have anything to do with him either. Even though they'd missed out on so much time together growing up, they quickly formed a bond as adults.

He's nothing like the selfish brat we remembered him as being. I've spoken to him, too, and he seems to really have it together; despite being raised by Renaldo during many of his formative years. He moved to Florida and is co-owner of one of the most popular Nuevo Latino restaurants there. He's made plans to visit Rosie within the next few weeks.

Raul rarely sees Tia Lupe. Since his move to Florida, their main contact is through phone. He told me that he loves his mother, but he can't understand the decisions she's made. Tia Lupe has been estranged from most of the family since Renaldo had her cut off contact with them years ago; especially when they tried to intervene and get her to leave him and bring Rosie back home. My parents have reconciled with her. But I doubt that the one person she wants most to be in her life again ever will be. I do believe that Tia Lupe is genuinely sorry for what she did, but she has to realize the pain that it has caused Rosie and it's a pain that I don't think Rosie will ever get over.

CHAPTER THREE / *Tres*

Chico has set up the tables and chairs in the backyard. I remember that we'll need more ice for the tub of beverages, so I call Rosie on her cell and ask her to stop by the store and pick some up. About half an hour after I've started getting the food prepped, I hear the doorbell. I'm about to answer the door when Chico comes back into the kitchen from downstairs.

"I'll get it. You concentrate on the important stuff; like the food."

"Oh, gee. Thanks."

He heads toward the living room. I hear a female voice laughing. I recognize the voice as that of our friend Crystal. We all met Crystal in high school. After her parents divorced, she and her mother moved here. She was a former army brat, who, before her parents split, had spent some time in Europe. I don't know if it was the time abroad or what, but Crystal had such an air of sophistication about her. We met her freshman year and she was fourteen going on twenty-five.

She seemed more suited for an Ivy League college than an urban high school. Her mother was a former Fashion Fair model and she'd passed on her sense of style to her daughter. Though her mother didn't make a lot as a private tutor, every summer, she managed to take Crystal to New York where she would get a few choice designer outfits for school in the fall. Crystal also inherited her mother's model looks—thank goodness. When Crystal first showed me a picture of her father, I couldn't help but think that he looked like a human frog. I remember playing it off by saying something along the lines of, "My, he looks distinguished in his uniform."

Although the females of our group held our own in the looks department, we lacked Crystal's sophistication and style, and therefore were thoroughly intimidated when we first met her. We instantly pegged her as "siddity." When we'd see her walking down the hall, Rosie would smirk and say, "Here comes the Queen of Detroit."

I was the first to get to really know her because we ended up sitting next to each other in Basic Economics. I've found that though she's a bit reserved at first, once she gets to know you, she's warm and personable. We gradually went from exchanging polite hellos, to notes, to finally being separated by Mrs. Gibson for talking too much. Crystal used to go home for lunch, until one day I invited her to come join us in the cafeteria, which she did from then on. That's when Rosie, Chico, Mario and Rhonda got to know her as well and she became part of our group.

Crystal is actually the person that Rosie is carrying a torch for. Rosie confided in me a few years ago that she had feelings for Crystal. She never let Crystal know because she knew Crystal was straight and wouldn't be at all receptive to her. She's managed to keep her feelings well-hidden and no one has picked up on it; except for Rhonda. Rhonda had noticed something and asked me if Rosie liked Crystal "in that way." I played coy and said I didn't know. She looked at me and said that I'd answered her question. But, she's kept her suspicions to herself.

Last year she moved from Detroit to one of the suburbs to be closer to her job as a Project Manager for a telecommunications company. We don't see her as often, and when we do, we never miss the opportunity to rib her about it.

For the past three years, she's been involved off and on with this guy named Shawn. He's a male dancer she met when Rosie invited us all to a party she was throwing at a club. There were male and female dancers providing entertainment—all of them handpicked by Rosie. Shawn and Crystal ended up striking up a conversation and hit it off. It was around this time that Rosie first started falling for Crystal, and she was sick as hell when she found out that Crystal had a new man; thanks to her indirectly.

As of a month ago, he and Crystal are broken up—for the fiftieth time. One night when we were hitting some trees, Crystal told me the main thing that makes her keep getting back with him is he's amazing in bed. She said that he was very freaky and introduced things to her that brought out the freak in her. He was very persuasive and she ended up trying all kinds of things—and finding out that she enjoyed them.

She wasn't high enough to elaborate on what these things were. That's how Crystal is—she'll share only so much of what's going on in her life. I love her and I consider her one of my best friends, but sometimes I feel like I don't really know her. She has this secretive air about her that borders on sneaky. Though she's mainly played the saintly role, we've heard so many rumors from mostly reliable sources about Crystal sleeping with this guy or that one, that we know at least some of it's true.

Crystal enters the kitchen with a yellow gift-wrapped box. Chico's following behind her, carrying a foil-covered pan. Crystal's about 5'5" and curvaceous with flawlessly smooth, dark cocoa skin. Her eyes are slightly slanted and she has full, pouting lips. Her hair used to be shoulder-length until recently, when she cut it— opting for a short Halle Berry-type do. She's wearing a pair of red silk Capri pants trimmed with gold; a matching halter top; and gold, jewel-encrusted sandals.

"Good, just in time to peel some onions for me."

"Hello to you, too." She pecks me on the cheek.

"How you doing, Mami? Looking beautiful, as usual."

"Thank you. I'm doing good. Hanging in there, girl." She puts the box on the kitchen table.

"That's good. What's that in the pan? Lee finished cooking the ribs already?"

"No, that's some chicken he cooked last night. He's going to hit me up on my cell when the ribs are ready to be picked up."

"That was so sweet of him to give us this also. He already wouldn't accept any money for the ribs."

"Yeah, he's a good one. I told Mom she'd better not let this one get away. He's ready to marry her, if she'd give the green light."

"Dang, don't tell me after all these years, your dad still has her turned off to marrying again?"

"Yes. She's straight-up paranoid that every man she gets with is going to turn into my drill sergeant daddy and start ordering her around. Chico! Get out of that chicken."

I glance over at Chico, who's holding a wing, looking like a little boy who'd been caught with his hand in the cookie jar. I go over, take the pan, and set it on the table in the kitchen nook.

"Yeah, you stay out of this chicken," I say as I turn around with a small drumstick. "This is for the shower."

"You're as bad as he is," Crystal says. "I might as well get me a piece, too."

"This is so good; even cold," says Chico.

"Um-hmm," I say, nodding my head in agreement.

"Hey, Nik. I noticed Rosie's car wasn't in the driveway. Where is she?"

"She went to take her friend home and to pick up the cake and some ice."

"Which friend is this? Anyone I know?" she asks as she nibbles on a wing.

"No. She's been calling here for a couple of weeks now. But Chico and I only met her this morning. We only spoke for a quick second, but she seems pretty nice; very soft-spoken. I think she used to dance at the club Rosie's at. She seems too shy to have been a dancer."

"Oh, I remember Rosie mentioning something about going back to dancing. When did she go back?"

"Last month."

"Last month? Boy, I've been out of the mix."

"That's what happens when you leave the 313 and move out to Buck Fuck Egypt," Chico teases.

"Come on. Bloomfield Hills isn't all that far from here. It's not like I'm living up in Sault Ste. Marie or something."

"Well, you might as well be," I say. "We hardly see you anymore. We miss you."

"Awww. I miss you guys also. I still drop through every two weeks to get my hair done. But shoot, I've been so busy that I have to head back right after my appointment. I promise to make it by here more often."

"You'd better. Hey, Chico, you haven't set up the stereo outside yet, have you?"

"No, why?"

"Can you throw sounds on?"

"Sure, DJ Chico at your service. What do you wanna hear?"

"Some old school. Dramatics or Earth, Wind and Fire or something."

"You got it." Chico gets up and heads for the living room. A minute or two later, we hear "Golden Time of Day" by Frankie Beverly and Maze.

"Heyyyy!" Crystal and I exclaim together. We wave our hands from side to side and sing along with it for a minute.

"All right, Crys. You're looking purdy and all, but I need you to chop some onions up for me, please."

"Sure." She gets a knife from the block and starts in on the onions I have near the sink. "You know, I'm going to have to go check Rosie out one night."

"Yeah, Chico and I went and it's a classy joint. Most of the customers are suits. If I had the guts, I'd dance, too, to make some money. That girl brings home more in one night than I bring home in a week."

"She certainly has the body for it."

"Her boss was glad when she came back since a lot of the customers were still asking about her."

"So what's up with her and Alejandro?"

"Nothing much. I was telling Chico that she needs to give him a chance. He's fine, intelligent, and sweet and has his own business. The brother's got it going on. Why are you asking, heifer? You want to fill out an application with him?"

"Could you blame me?" She grins. "No, I'm simply curious. I think she's a fool for passing his fine ass up. Is Rosie serious about this Lisa?"

"Lori, you mean. No, it's just a thing."

"I heard about the fling she had with Yvette, the girl from Hairy Situations."

"How did you hear about it?"

"From Yvette herself. She told me when she did my hair a few weeks back, when Cheryl was on vacation."

"For real? She told you?"

"Yep."

"I'm surprised. I thought she would've kept that secret in her little closet—so to speak. Especially the way she used to sneak over here late at night; parking down the street and shit. And leaving before the sun cracked the sky."

"Well, for some reason, she let the cat out of the bag to me."

"No, she did that to Rosie."

"Oh, hush. Anyway, from what she said, Rosie turned her out. She kept talking about how good Rosie was in bed. I had to tell her to shut up; she was going on about it so much."

"I guess Rosie did turn her out, the way she was always calling wanting to see Rosie. But you know Rosie can't stand to be smothered. Speaking of *la diabla.*" Rosie has gotten back and is walking toward the kitchen carrying the cake.

"Rosie, set that down in here in the nook."

"You got it. Chico, get the ice out the car for me," she says over her shoulder. "Hi there, Miss Thang, Miss all out in the 'burbs, Miss don't hardly see her peeps no more."

"Here we go," says Crystal.

Rosie puts the cake down on the table and comes back and gives Crystal a hug. "Good to see you, baby."

"Good to see you, too, sweetie. Sorry I can't hug you right back. I've got onions on my hands."

"That's okay. We don't see nearly enough of you, you know."

"Yes, I know. Nikki and Chico have already gotten on me. I had to make that move and get that apartment when it became available; it's less than five minutes from my job. I can actually walk to work, weather permitting. And I sure as heck don't miss tackling that freeway for the commute every morning."

"I hear you. Just don't forget about your peeps here in the city."

"That's not gonna happen." She gives Rosie a peck on the cheek.

"Nik, what do you want me to do with this ice?" Chico asks. "There's no room in this freezer."

"I think there's some room in the freezer downstairs. You can put it there for now."

"Okay," he says, heading down the stairs.

"Crystal, come to my room for a minute. I want to show you the pictures I took."

"Rosie," I say. "Crystal doesn't wanna see your freaky *Penthouse* pics."

"Shut it up. And they're not for *Penthouse*; they're for *Playboy*." She makes a face and sticks her tongue out at me. I do the same right back. She turns back to Crystal. "A photographer friend of mine took them and I'm going to send them to ole Hefner. I want you to help me pick the best ones."

"Okay, let me wash these onions off my hands first." Crystal heads toward the sink.

"You need to be helping me out in here. I realize you hate to cook, but don't be trying to duck and dodge. Not today."

"I ain't ducking and dodging nothing. Come on, Crystal, it'll only take a minute. We'll be back, Dickie."

"You'd better."

A few minutes later the phone rings. It's Rhonda.

"Hey, mommy-to-be."

"Hey, girl. What's going on?"

"Slinging pots. What's up with you? How you feeling?"

"I'm beat. This youngun had me up half the doggone night kicking. To top it off, our a/c went out this morning and no one can come out until Monday. I'm hot as hell."

"It's not that hot yet."

"Shoot, I'm hot. Lugging this extra weight, child, it could be 40 degrees and I'd be sweating. Anyway, what else is going on over there, other than you cooking? Is Rosie helping you?"

I sample some *chorizo* that I've finished cooking. "She shupposhed to," I mumble through a full mouth.

"What did you say? Get the dick out your mouth."

It's so funny, I almost spit out the food. "I said, she's supposed to. She's upstairs showing Crystal those nude pics she took."

"What, is Rosie trying to turn her on or something?"

We both giggle.

"Your cousin's still sniffing after Crystal, huh?"

"You ain't said nothing but a thang. Oh, I forgot, my lips are supposed to be sealed."

"Keep 'em sealed all you want. Mama knows what the dealy is. I wouldn't be surprised if Crystal lets her do more than sniff."

"Huh?" I pause from seasoning some ground beef. "Crystal? No, she's strictly dickly like us. Hell, quiet as she tries to keep it, she's gets more dick than we do."

"Hmm."

"I never picked up on anything. What makes you think that?"

"I wouldn't be surprised if she wasn't so strictly dickly and had a little licky in her."

"You're crazy! I don't know. If Rosie thought she had even an iota of a chance she wouldn't be able to contain herself. I'm sure her gaydar would've picked up some little blip. But then again, you never really know what's going on with Crystal."

"Okay, girl. I'm about to tell you something that I've been wanting to tell you for a while. But you've got to promise not to tell anybody, all right?"

"Yeah. What is it?" I stop seasoning the meat all together.

"You can't even tell Rosie. You guys tell each other everything, but you can't spill this. When Rosie gets high, she starts yapping. If she finds this out, I want it to be on her own. I don't want it to get traced back to me 'cause Dante told me to keep it to myself."

"Okay. I won't say anything."

"All right. If Rosie hasn't picked up anything on her gaydar, as you say, about Crystal, she needs to get it repaired."

"What do you mean?"

"You know Dante's friend Omar?"

"Uh-huh."

"His brother Jalil is married to this woman named Sheri. Crystal met them at this year's New Year's Eve party. Jalil and Sheri live not too far from Crystal. Well, Crystal and Sheri had been hanging pretty tight, going shopping and stuff together. Omar told Dante that Jalil got sick at work and went home early and caught Sheri and Crystal in bed together."

"What?! Get the fuck outta here!"

"I swear."

"Girl, you are *ly-ing!* You sure this hasn't gotten twisted somehow? You know once a story goes through a couple of people it gets..."

"Come on now, shit ain't gonna get that twisted. Omar's brother called him crying, girl. He said he 'kicked that dyke bitch wife of his out of his house.' And if he sees Crystal again, woman or not, he's gonna bust her face."

"I can't believe this. I never thought Crystal would... When did all this happen?"

"This was a little over a month ago. Dante said that Jalil let Sheri move back in the house last week."

"Oh my God." I stop and look to the dining room and make sure no one's in there. "You know," I whisper. "Crystal was telling me about this chick Yvette that works at Hairy Situations. Yvette and Rosie had a little fling a while back. Crystal said Yvette was telling her all the details. And I thought that was a bit odd because Yvette was really paranoid about anybody finding out, you know? When she came over here, she would park all down the street and leave first thing in the morning; even though people could just as easily assume she was kicking it with Chico. So I was wondering why she would all of a sudden be telling everything to Crystal—about how Rosie was in bed and stuff."

"Uh-huh. Obviously she knows what's up and probably something's going on between them."

"You think Crystal is bi or something?"

"I don't know. Crystal has always been a freak on the sneak. Always pretending she didn't really have sex, but it was steady getting back to us about her and some dude screwing."

"Yeah, that's true."

"That's my girl and all but she's always been an undercover ho."

"Uh-huh. At least we did our fucking on top of the covers. We never tried to perp on our shit. We ain't hoes but, at the same time, we ain't trying to hide that we do our thing."

"You know. She's a major ass freakazoid."

"Shit, we're freaks, too. We just don't freak like that."

"I know that's right. It's one thing if you want to keep certain things private, even from your friends, but it's another to try and play the virginal role when you know you ain't nowhere near being like that."

"What do you mean, 'keep certain things private even from your friends?' You got some skeletons in your bedroom closet, *chica?*"

"I might have a few bones rattling from the hangers."

"Like what?"

"Like none of your business, heifer." She snickers. "But all my skeletons are heterosexual ones."

"No doubt." I giggle. "Rosie would have a heart attack if she knew about Crystal."

"All right now. You promised."

"Oh, I'm not going to say anything. I hope that Rosie doesn't find out."

"Why?"

"'Cause she'll waste her time mooning after Crystal even more. You can't pick somebody for someone else, but I want her to give Alejandro a chance. If she and Rosie do something, that's gonna make Rosie fall in love with her harder. Meanwhile Crystal has moved her freaky ass on, leaving Rosie behind hurt."

"So Rosie's in love with her?"

"Yeah, I might as well let the shit drop. She loves her."

"I knew something was up. I didn't know it was that deep."

"Unfortunately. That's our friend, but if she hurts my cousin…"

"Well, nothing's happened up until now. Hopefully, shit will stay like that."

"I'm crossing my fingers. You know, I suddenly thought of something."

"Huh?"

"Girl, one time Crystal was over right after we moved in here. And Rosie had some girl visiting and Crystal's all, 'How can Rosie be with another girl? She can't do anything a man can't do. It doesn't make me feel any differently about Rosie, but I don't get it.'"

I hear Rhonda suck her teeth. "Like I said, I love her, but she's so fake at times. You should've known something was up then. How many times have one of us talked about doing or trying something and she'd be like, 'Eww, that's nasty,' and then we'd hear about her doing the same thing? She always screwed in our circles, so shit always got back to us."

"Mmm-hmm. That's her, girl."

"Like when we were talking about oral sex and I hadn't done it yet and I was getting tips from Rosie. She acted like she was so disgusted. Next thing you know, we heard she was giving head to that dude Elliot."

"I remember. He was bragging to Chico about it."

"Anyway, to change the subject. You know I appreciate y'all putting this shower together for me. I really do."

"Rhonda, it's the least we could do for you and my niece."

"You all are my real family. My other so-called family has called one by one, with lame excuses of why they can't make it."

"That's fucked up."

"Tell me about it. It's cool. They haven't been a part of my life all these years. I only put them on the invitation list because Ma wanted me to try one more time to reach out to them. She was hoping they'd changed over the years or something. And they haven't. It worked out for the best because I wouldn't want those people around my child anyway."

"It's their loss."

"Damn straight. But my cousin Kirsten, the only one that's got some sense, said that she would try to make it. She has to work, so she'll attempt to get off early. She said if she doesn't come, she'll drop off a gift to me on Sunday."

"That's good. She's real cool. I hope she can make it. I haven't seen her in a minute."

"Yep. It's hard for her, working two jobs and going to school."

"Have you heard from your father?"

"My biological one, or my real one?"

Her mother's second husband raised Rhonda. She's very close to him and considers him her real father. He and her mother separated over a year ago. A short time later, his job transferred him to Chicago. Her "biological" father left her and her mother when Rhonda was four years old. She's probably only seen him a dozen times since then. Even so, when Rhonda's stepfather wanted to legally adopt her, he wouldn't give his consent.

"If you're talking about my real one, yeah. He's doing better since the surgery. He's getting around now with the help of a cane. Ma's still there looking after him. I told her not to try to make it back for the shower and that looking after Dad was more important. I think those two are going to get back together. I'm crossing my fingers."

"I'll cross mine, too. I don't know why they got separated, as much as they love each other."

"'Cause they're both stubborn as hell, that's why. I can tell Ma likes Chicago, and it's only a few hours' drive, so she can see the baby often. Now as for my other so-called father, I haven't talked to his ass since he made me so mad when I finally called to tell him about the baby."

"You don't need that negative energy around you and your baby anyway; especially when he starts talking junk."

"I know that's right. 'Cause Dante had to really calm me down that night. So anyway, girl, I'm going to get my ass unstuck from this couch and take a bath. Dante and I will be over soon and I can help you out."

"The hell you will. This is your day—you and the baby's. When you get your white ass over here, all you're gonna do is eat, drink lemonade, and open your gifts. You hear?"

"You don't have to tell me a second time. I was only saying that to be nice 'cause, honey, I'm feeling too fat and lazy to do anything."

"You take it easy before you come over here."

"I will, girl."

"I'm still in shock over what you told me. But, at the same time, I'm not shocked. You know?"

"I hear you. I felt the same way when Dante told me. We always said that we wouldn't put anything past Crystal and we were right."

"Mmm-hmm. Anyway, I'll see you later, heifer."

"All right. Bye-bye."

Rosie and I met Rhonda the summer we moved here. One day we were walking to the store when we saw two girls—one white and one black—fighting on some-one's lawn. The white girl was sitting on the black one's chest, raining her with blows. The black girl had her arms up, trying to block the hits.

"Dang-ee!" Rosie exclaimed. "That girl's getting her butt kicked!"

We walked closer and stood, looking on in awe, a few feet away.

"Now you leave me alone! Understand?" said the white girl. She'd stopped hitting the other girl and was pointing her finger in her face. The black girl didn't say anything. The white girl hit her again. "I said, do you understand?"

"Yeah," the girl said weakly.

The white girl got up off the girl and stood. The black girl scooted back, got up, and took off running down the street. The white girl brushed the dirt off her blue overalls. She looked up at us warily.

"What're you staring at me for?"

Rosie and I looked at one another for a second.

"No reason," I said. Rosie and I walked closer. "My name's Nikki and this is my sister Rosie." Rosie and I had decided to tell everyone that we were sisters because when we said we were cousins, inevitably questions about her parents would be asked. If later on we wanted to tell them the truth, then we would. People naturally assumed we were sisters anyway because we looked a lot alike. I was a bit darker. If someone questioned how we could be sisters and be only four months apart, we said that we were half-sisters. It helped that we had the same last name.

"My name's Rhonda."

Rhonda appeared to be our age. She had her long dark brown hair in two braids, though it was tousled from her altercation. She was cute and she had pretty bluish-green eyes.

"Why were you and that girl fighting?" Rosie asked.

"Her boyfriend Javon kissed me at my friend Ebony's birthday party and after he kissed me, he asked me to be his girlfriend. Then she found out and told me she was his girlfriend so I broke up with him, but she's still been picking with me; even though I told her I didn't know he had a girlfriend and don't like him no more. Today, when I was walking from the park, she started trying to fight with me, so I finally let her have it," she said breathlessly.

I noticed she was twirling her neck as she spoke, the way Rosie and I did. I'd never seen a white girl do that before.

"Oh," Rosie and I said together.

"Rosie and I beat up this boy the other day," I said with pride.

"Yeah. He kept picking with us so we gave it to him good," added Rosie. "He was bleeding all over the place."

"Wow. Y'all beat up a boy?"

"Yep, sure did," I said.

"And you made him bleed?"

"Uh-huh," said Rosie as she then twirled her neck and flipped her hand. "He hasn't messed with us since. Him or his brother."

"Y'all live around here? I've never seen you."

"We live two streets over," answered Rosie. "We moved here last month."

"We're from New York," I added, offering further proof that we also were bad asses. I could tell that she was just as impressed with us as we were with her.

"How old are you guys?"

"Seven," I answered.

"Me, too. How old was the boy you beat up?"

"I think he's eight or nine," said Rosie.

"And he's a big boy, too. Right, Rosie?"

"Yeah, he's really big. He looks like a fourth- or fifth-grader."

"Wow. Boys are hard to beat up," said Rhonda.

"Yep, they sure are," I said. "But we did it with no problem."

"I go to Emerson. Is that where you guys are going when school starts?"

"Yeah," I answered. "In New York we went to Catholic school, but my—our mother—said it doesn't make sense to go to one here when we got a good regular school right down the street. Our father has been fussing, saying that he wants us to still go to Catholic school."

"Oh, so you think y'all gonna end up going to Catholic school?"

"No, we'll be going to Emerson," Rosie and I said in unison. We knew who ran things in our house.

"Hey, you wanna go to the store with us?" asked Rosie. "We're gonna get some Now or Laters, sunflower seeds and stuff."

"I don't have any money," said Rhonda, patting her pockets.

"We have enough to get you something," I said.

"Okay, thanks."

After seeing the way she lit into that girl, Rhonda won my and Rosie's instant respect. Back in New York the few white kids in our neighborhood were usually on the receiving end of an ass-whipping. We knew that this was one tough girl and she'd be a great ally. Rhonda quickly became more than an ally; she became our friend.

She'd moved into the neighborhood when she was six years old. Her mother had remarried and Rhonda's stepfather was black. Being the only white kid on the block and one of only a few in school, she was an easy target for bullies and wannabe-bullies. Her stepfather would take her into the backyard to hone her fight skills on an upright punching bag and he'd coach her on her swing. Her mother, at first, objected to these lessons because she thought it was teaching her violence. But after Rhonda had gotten beat up at the playground and had come home in tears and bruised, she relented. The fighting lessons gradually paid off and Rhonda soon got the reputation of being someone not to be messed with.

Most of her mother's family didn't approve of her mother's marriage and had little contact with Rhonda as a result. Whenever she did go to visit her relatives, she'd come home upset because they put down the way she dressed, spoke, and the music she listened to as being "black." She and her mother decided she wouldn't go back to visit again when some of her cousins ganged up on her and said she and her mother were nigger lovers. Her cousin Kirsten was the only one who stood up for her. Her mother was married to a Samoan man and she was picked on, too.

Rhonda's biological father was no different. The handful of times that she'd seen him over the years, he'd used the opportunities to say hateful, racist things about her stepfather that resulted in Rhonda getting into heated arguments with him. Rhonda's mother found this a tad ironic since she'd learned following their divorce that he'd carried on a two-year affair with a black woman during their marriage.

Rhonda has dated black men almost exclusively. She dated one white guy she met on her job until he told her she'd be perfect if she didn't "act so black." And she went with Enrique, my and Rosie's cousin, when he spent a summer here from New York. Rhonda's now pregnant by Dante—her boyfriend of four years. She met him up north at an Indian-run casino.

It was an appropriate place for them to have met, considering Dante has a colossal-sized gambling problem. But by the time Rhonda found out, she'd already fallen in love. She refuses to leave him; despite all the problems his addiction has caused in their relationship. Rhonda works as a city auditor and her job pays well, but Dante's gambling has put a tremendous strain on their finances. Rhonda's very intelligent but, for some stupid reason, she opened a joint account with Dante. So my eyebrow didn't raise a centimeter when she called me crying about how he'd drained the account when he'd gone on a gambling spree at the Windsor Casino. Rhonda had just put a crap-load of bills in the mail, so if you stuck your head out the window, you could hear the "boing" sound of checks bouncing all around the city of Detroit and the surrounding suburbs as a result.

I think the most foul thing was what he did right before Rhonda found out she was pregnant. Dante's car was in the shop, so he took Rhonda to work in her car and used it for the day. After he picked her up from work, they arrived back home to find it had been burglarized. Rhonda was about to get on the phone to call the police when she noticed something. There was only broken glass on the outside of the door where the burglars had supposedly broken in. If someone had broken into the house, glass should've been inside. She confronted Dante and after almost an hour of hollering and screaming at him, he finally confessed that he'd staged the entire thing. When she asked where the stuff was, he said he'd pawned it. The next day she made him take her to the pawnshops and she had enough money to get most of the things. The so-called "burglary" had taken place early in the day and, by that time, Dante had already gambled most of the money away. She kicked him out for a whopping three days before taking him back.

She said her reason for staying is that when you love someone, you gotta take the good with the bad. I think she's taking that to the extreme, but she refuses to listen to me, Rosie, or anyone. We gave up on even trying to say anything; especially when we found out she was pregnant. If she hadn't left Dante before, she sure as hell wasn't going to leave him now.

I'm about to go and get Rosie when I spot her and Crystal coming through the dining room. Rosie's changed into a halter-top.

"Quit biting off Crystal," I say to her as she enters the kitchen.

"Zip it. I was already thinking of wearing a halter today. So there."

"You should put on one, too, Nikki," says Crystal. "Like in the old days, when we'd all dress alike sometimes."

"Naw. Rhonda might feel left out if she comes over and sees the three of us in halters and she's rocking some *muumuu*."

"That's true," says Rosie.

"She's put on quite a few then?" asks Crystal.

"Yeah. I spoke with her right after you two went upstairs. She feels really uncomfortable. It must be extra hard carrying a baby in the summer."

"Really," Crystal says.

Chico comes in from outside.

"The stereo is set up and ready to be blasted."

"Thanks, Chico," I say. "You've been a great help." I look over at Rosie, "Unlike some people."

She gives me the finger. "What do you want me to do?"

"Get the shrimp ready for the *mofongo*. I cleaned most of them last night, but the ones I didn't are in the refrigerator in that green bowl on the top shelf."

Rosie reaches in the fridge and gets the bowl of shrimp out.

"Hey, guys, I'll go and put up the decorations," says Crystal. "I want to do something, and you know I'm useless in the kitchen."

Who is she telling? I had to re-chop that onion she called herself dicing up for me. I tell her that the decorations are in some Party City bags up in my room. She gets them and goes outside to put them up.

CHAPTER FOUR / Quatro

Almost everything is cooked and people have started streaming in. Chico should be back any time now from picking up Mario. Crystal got the call from Lee that the ribs are ready. She asked Rosie to go with her to pick them up. I add deejay to my list of duties and program some sounds. I'm greeting people, placing the gifts on the gift table, and putting out food and drinks on the food table. I'm in the kitchen about to take some bottled water outside when our friend Odell comes in carrying a white casserole dish.

Odell's originally from Atlanta and is as gay as a pool party at Boy George's house. We met him a few years ago when he started working at the salon that we go to get our hair done. He's of medium height and build. He has a dark brown complexion and medium-length hair that he has braided into cornrows. He's average-looking; nowhere near Shemar Moore but he's not ugly either. He's wearing white jeans and a light blue shirt. I make a mental note to set a nail appointment when I see his perfectly done French-manicured nails. Something that can always be heard from us when he's around is, "You're so crazy!" He's quite a character and will amuse you; even when he doesn't mean to.

"Hi, sweetheart! Georgia Power's in the house—bringin' the electricity!" He leans in and gives me a peck on the lips.

"Hey, crazy. Mmm." I smack and lick my lips. "Is that some kind of flavored lip balm I'm tasting?"

"Yes, it is, child—grape. I keeps my lips moist and sweet." He puts the dish down on the counter. "Girl, I seen all the food on the table out there and you still got some to take out. You been a cooking fool, I see."

"Um-hmm. Not all of the dishes are mine. A few people brought something."

"That cousin of yours hide from the pots as usual?"

"Man, everybody knows how she is. She did at first, but she ended up helping. Even though she doesn't like to, she's a good cook. Right now she's gone with Crystal to pick up some ribs. They should be back any time now."

"Oh no, not ribs. Chile, I been tryin' to be a vegetarian but I see I ain't gonna be one today, 'cause I love me some ribs."

"You've been saying you're going vegetarian since I've known you. You know your ass ain't giving up beef."

"I didn't say my ass was giving up beef. I said I was..."

We both break out giggling.

"Anyway, Odell. Where's Robert?"

He sucks his teeth. "Who knows, girl. Roberta probably on her knees behind some garbage cans. I don't know and I don't care. Okay?"

"Trouble in paradise?"

"Yes, but trouble ain't nothin' new. I'm about to pack it up on him this time. We got into it real bad the other night."

"What about?"

"He always harping on me to butch up. I keep telling him I've been this way all my life and at 34—and looking 24, thank you—I ain't trying to change for no damn body. He wanna maintain his little macho front 'cause he think that's gonna make him more accepted by folks, then he can go right on ahead. But shit, let a diva be a diva, you know?"

"I hear you. You've always been this way, and if he had a problem with it, he should've stepped right from jump."

"Thank you!" He gives me a high-five. "You can't be anybody but yourself. Either people gonna accept you for what you is or they ain't. Ain't no use in you trying to mold yourself to be who you think they want you to be. 'Cause they damn sho ain't gonna be who you want them to be."

"Preach on it."

"But he went and crossed the damn line. Do you know he had the nerve to say that I was a 'stereotypical fag' and that if I didn't act the way I do, those mens probably wouldn't have jumped me last spring?"

"No he didn't!"

"Yes, he did, chile. He was wrong for that. He knows that I went through a thing when that there happened and for him to say that, I just looked at him and the look I was givin' must've told the tale, 'cause he gonna hurry up and try to backtrack on what he said. But it was too late. So anyway, next! I'm making some plans on the hush to move in with this little girl named Jamal when his brother goes away to college. I ain't told Robert, 'cause I don't want no drama. And he might try to get funky and make me leave before I'm ready to."

"That's true."

"He'll find out when his ass comes home to a couch and a 19-inch TV. Okay?"

"You're so wrong, Odell."

"The shit I am. I'm right as rain. He didn't hardly have nothin' in that shack when I first moved in. I'm the one who decorated it to the hilt and turned that little roach motel into the fabulous house it is now. That's right, me and my..." he said, moving his head from side to side for emphasis, "'...stereotypical fag ass.' You best believe I'm gonna take *everythang* I brought up in there—every pot and pan, fork and spoon, pilla and pillacase. I don't care if it's a tissue roll with half a square stuck to it. If I bought it, it's going on the truck."

I chuckle. "You are too crazy!"

"Don't be laughing, Nikki Morena. It ain't funny." He folds his arms, rolls his eyes, and grins.

Odell has a habit of sometimes replacing O's with A's in people names. Like saying Morena instead of Moreno and calling Alejandro, Alejandra.

"Odell, what Robert said was wrong, but are you sure you want to leave him?"

"Hell yes. Thangs ain't been right between us in a while and this last little incident was the last straw. Besides, I shoulda done been gone. The worst thing you can do is stay with somebody who try to change who you is. Now if my momma, a go to church every Sunday, Southern Baptist, can accept me for who I am and how I am, then who is the Negro to try and tell me to change?"

"I agree, but I hate to see you two break up for good. He does love you, Odell. But I understand where you're coming from. What's this Jamal all about? Where did you meet him?"

"At Mr. Alan's. He's a little thugalicious thing. He was in there with his boys gettin' some shoes. He slipped me his number. And a few nights later he slipped me somethin' else."

"You're silly."

"I see you cutting your eyes to the banana pudding. You might as well hurry up and get some. I brought it straight on in here, so you could have first dibs."

"Thanks, hon. I realize it's rude to dig in before the guests, but bump that."

I get a spoon and bowl and scoop a little banana pudding into it.

"This is delicious," I say after a bite.

Odell gets a spoon and dips into my bowl.

"It sho is good. Didn't I throw down?"

"Mmm-hmm."

After I finish, we take the rest of the dish, along with the water, outside and set it on the table. As we do so we see Rhonda and Dante coming into the backyard. Rhonda is looking tired—poor thing. She doesn't have the glow that pregnant women are said to have. Although she's tried to stay out of the sun as much, she's managed to get somewhat of a tan. She's about 5'4" and normally weighs about 115 pounds, but the pregnancy has added at least 50 pounds to her frame. She's wearing a blue denim dress that, frankly, looks like a tent. She has her hair cut into a short bob. Still, she looks lovely.

"Ooohhh, chile," whispers Odell. "Miss Rhonda looking like a beached whale, ain't she?" I nudge his side with my elbow. "You know I'm spittin' truth. Mmm. That boyfriend of hers sho' do look good."

"Instead of being at this shower, his ass needs to be sipping on coffee and eating stale pastries at a Gamblers Anonymous meeting. That's the best gift he could give Rhonda and the baby."

"You ain't neva lied."

Odell and I wait until they've finished greeting some of the guests before we walk over to them.

"*Hola*, Mami." I give Rhonda a warm hug.

"Hi, Nikki. Look at all the gifts—I mean guests." She giggles.

"You were right the first time." I chuckle. I look at Dante. "Hi, Dante," I say in my most polite tone.

"Hi, Nikki. Man, I ain't never been to no baby shower and never thought I'd go, but this is sweet." He's bobbing his head to DMX coming out of the speakers and looking over at the food and gifts.

Rosie put the word out to some of the folks to give the receipts for the gifts directly to Rhonda; in case Dante tries to take them back for cash and go on a little gambling expedition. He's about my height, muscular build, with reddish-brown skin, dark sandy-colored hair and gray eyes. He's wearing a wife-beater, khakis and sandals. I hate to admit it, but he is handsome.

"Hello, precious," says Odell, giving Rhonda a hug. "Girl, you lookin' good! You just glowin'."

Rhonda smirks. "Now, Odell, I oughta slap you for lying."

Dante takes her hand and kisses it. "You know you're still beautiful."

"Both of you can lie to me all you want. I'm not complaining a bit."

"How you doing, Dante?" asks Odell.

"What's up?" Dante replies somewhat curtly.

Rhonda told me that Dante isn't homophobic. He doesn't mind gay women; it's just that he's not one to get warm and friendly with gay guys.

Dante and Rhonda go to greet the rest of the guests. I notice that the plastic-ware is getting low so I go inside to get some more. As I'm getting the utensils together, I notice someone walking through the dining room. It's Mario and Chico. They've entered from the front door. Chico is in front carrying Mario's two suitcases. I've been perfectly cool 'til this point, but now all of sudden I feel butterflies in my stomach.

"Hey, hey, hey," I say, smiling.

"Sup," says Chico. "The cars are piling up out there. We had to park down the street. I'll take these downstairs for you, bro'."

"Thanks, man."

Chico heads downstairs. He winks at me as he passes by. Mario and I stand there looking at each other, smiling. It's been a while so I'm drinking him in for a minute. Damn, he's so fine. Mario's about 6'2" and used to be on the slender side. But since he started weight training a few years back, his build is now medium and muscular. He has a neatly trimmed moustache and adorable jet-black curly hair and the most beautiful green eyes. They're like two emeralds. He's wearing black slacks and shoes, and a dark blue silk shirt. The California sun has darkened his skin from light to a dark golden shade.

We then walk toward each other. We don't say anything; just wrap our arms around each other in a warm, deep hug. After a few moments I move my head and give him a soft kiss on the lips and pull my head back and look into his eyes.

"Girl, you better quit playin'," he says with his sexy voice brimming with huskiness. He kisses me gently, yet firmly. I feel his tongue slip slowly into my mouth. My tongue greets his—swirling in a reunion dance. I'm instantly lost in our kiss, becoming wonderfully reacquainted with the warmth, feel and taste of his mouth. We hold each other even tighter as our kissing grows more fervent. We release soft moans into one another's mouth. I feel his hunger pressing against me. I take one hand from around his waist and move it up to his soft curly hair—running my fingers through it.

"Uh, sorry," we hear from behind us.

We break away from our kiss and turn around and see Chico. He's grinning at us from the doorway leading into the kitchen from the stairs.

"I figured you two were having a little reunion so I went straight outside after I put your bags up. But some of the fellas are about to riot if I don't get some more beer out there. Don't mind me." He whistles as he gets a case of Heineken out the bottom of the refrigerator. "Pretend I wasn't even here."

He looks at us, still grinning hard, and goes outside. Mario and I, our arms still wrapped around one another, are smiling after him. Chico closes both the door leading downstairs and outside and as well as the main door. That cuts down on the noise from outside immensely. Mario plants a kiss on my forehead, the tip of my nose and then my lips.

"I could stand here kissing you forever but I'm sure we'll be interrupted again."

"'Tis true." I reluctantly let him go. "It's so good to see you again."

"Same here. Still beautiful, I see."

"You don't look so bad yourself. Okay, let's cut to the chase—spill it. What's this surprise you said you had for me? And how is it that we're going to be blessed with your presence for the next two weeks? Ever since you left for L.A., the most you've been back home for has been three or four days a stretch."

"Well, the surprise and the reason I'm here for two weeks are connected."

"Come on, don't keep me in suspense."

"I quit my job at the bank. Because—dramatic pause."

"I'm about to kill you, Mario."

"Okay, I'll stop messing with you. I quit my job at the bank because I start a new one in two weeks. I'm going to be a writer at this magazine called *Urban Report*. Right now they're only situated on the West Coast but they're about to branch out nationally."

"Ahhhhhh!" I scream. I wrap my arms around his neck and plant kisses all over his face. "I'm so happy for you!"

"Thanks, baby. I'm happy, too. I wanted to tell you in person. The only reason I held on to that boring ass job was because I couldn't depend on the money from freelance work. It feels good to finally have a steady gig writing. The timing worked out great and everything 'cause I'm here for Rhonda's baby shower. Nik, are you crying, girl?"

"A little," I say as I wipe away a tear. "I'm so happy for you, Mario. You deserve this. You're so talented. I have every article you've written and I reread them all the time."

"You don't know how much your support means to me. It makes me even happier that you're so excited for me."

"Of course. This is what you've always wanted to do and you are."

"You know, I've got to do the damn thang." He makes a motion of popping his collar.

"Oh, brother," I say, smiling and rolling my eyes.

"Rosie and Chico both told me how you kicked ass in that last play."

"I did pretty good; if I do say so myself. I'm auditioning for another one next week. The part's small but meaty."

Mario grows silent and looks at me.

"What's up, Mario? You got another surprise for me?"

"No." He pauses for a second and then takes my hand. "Nik, in order for you to do the damn thing, you know you're going to have to make that move that we talked about."

"To New York or Los Angeles?"

"Yes. You're not interested in going back to New York, so your alternative is L.A. You've got me out there, so you're not going to be like a lot of other people who come out there not knowing a soul. I've got a two-bedroom, and hey, I could use a roommate. It's expensive as hell out there. I've made contacts through some of the interviews I've done freelancing. And I'm sure I'll make even more with this writing job. Now I'm not saying I can get you a five-picture deal, but I can at least put your name out to the right people and help you get your foot in the door."

"You'd do that for me?"

He looks at me dead serious. "That and more." With his other hand he strokes my cheek. "I'd do anything for you, Nik," he says softly.

I put my hand on top of his and then kiss his palm.

"I've got to make that move, and soon. I mean, at 26, a good portion of the industry already considers me over the hill and I'll have to shave about four years off my age." I sigh. "It's gonna be so hard leaving Rosie, Chico, and everybody." I look around. "And this house."

"It's not going to be easy. It wasn't easy for me. But I had to do what I had to do, and now it's your turn. Feel me?"

I stare down to the floor.

"Feel me?" he repeats, lifting my chin to look at him.

"Yes, I do."

"When I first went out there to go to school, it was hard as hell. I didn't know anyone. I couldn't call home and expect a sympathetic ear from my parents because they didn't want me to leave in the first place, but I made it through."

"I was so scared that you'd end up forgetting me, once you moved out there."

"Never."

"Oh, yeah." I grin. "You couldn't forget about me if you tried. You always remember your 'first one.'"

"Definitely. You were the first and the best."

"Come on. I couldn't still be the best. What did I know at seventeen? Certainly, you've been with women who were better and far more experienced."

"It's not all about knowing a million tricks and positions, Nik. That was a very special time; both of us experiencing lovemaking for the first time together. That was a hard act to follow."

"In more ways than one."

"You and your puns." He chuckles.

"Those were the days. All right, we have two whole weeks to reminisce. You'd better get out there and say hello to everybody. I didn't tell Rhonda you were coming. Her water might break at the surprise of seeing you."

"God, I hope not."

"Take these plastic utensils out for me when you go, please."

"Sure." He takes them from me.

"Thanks."

He leans in and gives me another kiss, tracing my lips with his tongue—sending sparks throughout my body. He gives me a final kiss on the forehead before heading outdoors. A few moments later I can hear Rhonda squeal with delight once Mario sets foot outside.

What a waste of time it was for Chico to set up downstairs for him. Mario's going to be in my bed; we both realize that. Why are we playin'?

Mario and I started to develop feelings that were deeper than our friendship when we were a junior and senior in high school, respectively. It was weird for us because we'd had a brother/sister type relationship up to that point. It seemed almost incestuous that we were becoming sexually attracted to one another. We both tried to ignore our growing attraction, but it grew stronger than any trepidation we had.

We had a special bond through our love of the arts; mainly music and movies. Other than drama class, my only other extracurricular activity was writing for the school paper. Mario wrote for it as well. I critiqued movies and he reviewed the latest music, as well as doing an occasional editorial. The two of us spent a lot of time together alone, outside of hanging with the others in our group.

We spent endless hours talking about our plans for the future. I was going to become a famous actress; he a respected, activist-minded journalist, and how we were going to combine our talents and write a screenplay together.

One night, all of the sexual energy that we'd been trying so hard to quell, exploded in such a way that we'd skipped all the bases and gone straight to the home plate. He'd just gotten back in town from a week's vacation in Las Vegas with his family. We were in his room listening to some music he was to review. We were on the floor; he was sitting up and I was lying on my back with one arm under my head.

"I'm not liking this," I said.

"Me neither. One of the main reasons he said he wanted to go solo was so he could branch out and do different music. Now he comes out with something that sounds exactly like the stuff his old group did—five years ago."

"Exactly. The one track that I halfway liked, he ruined by trying to do a rap."

"Yeah, he should've had a real rapper guest on that track and not do it himself."

"Um-hmm."

"What's up with you? You seem kind of distracted. Or has that piece of crap CD lulled you into a catatonic state?"

"It hasn't helped; that's for sure. Rosie and I did something and if my parents find out about it, they'll have a conniption. They'll probably ship us both to convents in San Juan or something."

"Oh man, what did you two she-devils do now?"

"We got tattoos."

"For real? Where and when?"

"Rosie kicks it with this guy who lives down near Mexican Town. His father's a tattoo artist and even though we're underage, he said if we swore we wouldn't rat him out, he'd hook us up. We got them last week."

"Day after I left, I bet."

I grinned. "Two days."

"See, I knew it. Man, every time I leave town you get into devilment." He lay back on his side next to me, propped up on his elbow, looking at me. "What am I going to do with you, Nikki?" Suddenly, I felt the current in the room change. "What did y'all get?"

"Rosie got a bouquet of roses with blood dripping from them and I got a unicorn with Zuzu written underneath it."

"Blood dripping? Never mind. I don't even want to know. Where did you get it?"

"I told you, down near Mexican Town. It was at this place off Bagley."

"I mean, where did you get the tattoo on your body, do-do."

"Oh. On my right thigh."

"Let me see."

"No."

"Why?"

"'Cause I still have it bandaged and, you know, it's on my thigh."

"So? Peel back the bandage a bit and let me peek. And so what if it's on your thigh. Like I ain't never seen your thigh before. We've gone swimming together how many times?"

"I don't care. I'm not ready for anybody to see it yet. Wait till it's completely healed."

"Nikki, you're going to be held captive in this room until you let me see it."

"Okay. Just make sure I get a shower a day and three square meals."

He moved closer to me. "Let me see it." His voice had a seductive tone to it. I could actually feel myself getting aroused from the sound of it.

I said nothing. I only held his gaze. All of my nerves were at attention—anticipating what I sensed was about to happen.

After a few moments, Mario put his hand on the waistband of my gray sweatpants. His eyes never left mine. His hand slid under the waistband and gently pulled it down. I didn't protest. Instead, I raised my hips so that he could pull them down. He brought my sweatpants to the top of my knees. His hand moved slowly back up my leg and rested on my belly. My heart wasn't beating as much as it was pounding. My mouth was devoid of moisture.

He leaned over and kissed me, lightly at first and then with increased intensity. I slid an arm under his waist and, with the other, I grabbed the back of his head and brought him into an even deeper kiss. I felt his hand move inside my panties; his middle finger stroked my vulva. I put my hand over his and guided his finger to my clit.

"Mmm, right there," I moaned. "A little softer, Mario. Yes, like that."

He started to nibble on my neck, which was extremely sensitive. The desire and good feeling raging through my body was more than I could stand. I took my panties and sweatpants completely off. Mario took his cue from me and removed his jeans, along with his underwear. I saw his hardened dick. I was amazed at its size, the length and girth of it. It scared me a little, but not enough to make me change my mind on what I was about to do. Mario peeled off his jersey and threw it to the side. He got up and walked over to his door and locked it. He dimmed the light a little. He came back over to me and reached out both his hands. I grabbed them and he pulled me up off the floor. He put his hands on my hips and kissed me again. I broke our kiss.

"When will your parents and Chico be back?"

"I locked the door, just in case. Chico's spending the night over our cousin's house and..." He kissed my neck. "My parents, they can play *euchre* for hours. They never get back from that before 10."

I glanced at the clock and saw that it was only 7:15. Mario took off my sweat-shirt and led me to the bed. He pulled back the covers and sat down. I stood in front of him. He looked down at the bandage pad covering my tattoo.

"I guess I can wait to look at that." He grinned at me.

I sucked my teeth and grinned back at him. I unhooked my bra and slipped it off. I tossed it on the floor. Mario looked at my breasts like he was mesmerized. He lay back in the bed and moved over. I got in beside him and lay on my back. He leaned over and took one of my breasts into his mouth. I'd been "felt up" by a couple of boys and when they'd touched my breasts it had felt good, but that was nothing compared to the sensation brought about by Mario's mouth on them. It sent intense shocks throughout my body. It was almost too much to take. He moved his head and began sucking on my other breast. I took his hardness into my hand and stroked it. Mario let out a moan. I glided my thumb across the head of it, feeling the wetness. He lifted his head up and looked at me.

"Nik, are you sure you want to do this?" he asked, breathing slightly hard.

"Yes, I'm sure. I'm positive."

"Okay, 'cause if you don't want to, right now is the time to let me know."

"I do, baby."

"I don't want to disappoint you, Nik. Other than working out my palm, I don't have any experience."

"I don't have any experience, either. So we'll learn what to do together."

"Wait a minute. You're a virgin, too? I thought maybe you and Terrance had done it when you went together last summer."

"Heck no. The only thing I gave that boy was blue balls. I tell you everything, so I would've told you if we'd done anything."

"I guess we're both rookies then." He chuckled.

I gave him a peck on the lips. He reached across me, over to his book bag on the floor beside the bed. He pulled out a roll of three condoms.

"Well, I see you're nice and prepared," I said.

"Don't trip. I got these yesterday when the lady from Planned Parenthood visited health class."

"Uhh, yeah," I teased.

He blushed. "For real, girl."

That night we ended up using all three condoms. The first time was kind of awkward because it was somewhat painful for me and Mario was so excited that he came within minutes. The second time was a little better but, by the third time, we'd found our little groove and though I didn't orgasm, it felt so good that it didn't matter.

The new turn in our relationship lasted until Mario left to finish college in L.A. four years later. We knew that we were entering into a new phase in our lives and that holiday and spring break visits weren't going to be enough to maintain our relationship. The week before he left, we tearfully decided to break off the romantic part of our relationship and remain friends. We've always kept in touch, through phone and email.

The couple of times that Mario has made it back home, either he was involved with someone or I was. The magnetic draw was still there, but we remained faithful to our respective mates. This is the first time that neither of us is in a relationship. In all raw honesty, I can't say that I didn't hope to one day be reunited with Mario. Just a few minutes ago, it was like we were never apart and had never been involved with other people. No man has captured my heart the way he did. And if there is such a thing as a soul mate, I believe that he is mine.

I suddenly feel like I've been hit with a kick in my hypocritical ass. I realize that from the beginning of my relationship with Jaime, I was the cheater—in my heart. I really wasn't all that justified in striking out at Jaime that night. Yeah, he crept around and hit the sheets with some skank, but I was the one secretly longing to be with someone else. In my eyes my infidelity was far worse than his. I'd be sick if I were involved with someone and the entire time they were carrying a torch for someone else and secretly wished to be with them. I'm not feeling too good, now that I've brushed away the sugar from my own shit. I'll think more about this later and put the guilt I'm feeling on hold because if I don't, I won't be able to enjoy this special day. I open a bottle of Negra Modelo and drink it in about four gulps.

CHAPTER FIVE / *Cinco*

I grab a case of Malta and a case of Negra Modelo and head back outside. Rosie and Crystal have gotten back with the ribs and the way folks are attacking those bones, you wouldn't think that there are over a dozen other dishes on the table. Rosie and Crystal are taking turns hugging Mario. Chico has taken over again as deejay.

"Chico, baby!" shouts Rosie. "Put some La India on, *por favor!*"

"Coming right up!"

As soon as one of India's songs starts, Rosie starts salsa dancing. Crystal and others follow her lead. I take the beverages over to the table and then walk over and grab Mario's hand.

"Nik, I'm not good at this."

"Please. Salsa dancing is all about knowing how to move your body; especially your hips. And, baby, from what I remember, you've got that down pat."

He grins and starts following my moves. He looks me in the eyes and takes one hand from mine and slips it around my waist. He pulls my body to his and moves his hips into mine.

"Like this?" he says in my ear.

"Oh, yeah. Like that."

I can feel that he already has an erection. He dips his hips low and rubs his hardness against my pubic area. I grind my pubic bone against his erect dick even harder, enjoying the feeling.

"Nik, baby, I'm gonna cream in my pants if we don't stop."

I grind even harder. Then the song skips and Chico goes to fix it. We stop dancing and Mario holds me close to him.

"Nikki, I ought to strangle you. If it wasn't for that song skipping, I would've busted one right here in front of everybody."

"You know you was loving it," I say, grinning.

"Of course I was loving it. That's why I almost busted one. Just don't move from in front of me for a few minutes. I've got a huge ass boner and I don't want to scare the horses."

"You wouldn't scare them, as much as you'd make 'em jealous."

"Boy, are you good for my ego."

Chico puts on another CD, a slow song by Marc Anthony.

"*Chevere,*" I say. "Here's a song where I can hold you close."

We begin to slow dance. I close my eyes. It feels so good to be back in Mario's arms again; wrapped up in his body, his scent and his vibe. Being with him now makes my breakup with Jaime seem like three years ago, instead of three months. Too soon for me, the slow song ends and the next one on is a funky hip-hop number by Slum Village.

"Well, that's that. Your deejaying brother knocked out the romantic flow. Let's go get some ribs before the vultures eat them all up."

"Okay."

Holding hands, we walk over to the table and fix our plates.

"This is the shit," Mario says after a bite of rib.

"Ms. Johnson's boyfriend made these. Crystal said he used to run a barbecue joint on the East Side. He needs to reopen another one 'cause most restaurants be playing with their ribs—throwing them in the oven."

"Ain't that the truth! If anything, he should come out to Cali. You don't know how hard it is to find good smoked ribs out there in Tofu Land."

Mario and I get some more of the other dishes and go sit down. Right then, Alejandro enters the backyard. He's standing there holding a gift, watching Rosie intently as she dances. Now here's another fine piece of man. Alejandro is 6 feet of gorgeous Cuban. His skin and hair coloring is very similar to Rosie's. His body is muscular like Mario's, only a bit thicker. He has warm, tender brown eyes and a boyishly handsome grin.

He's wearing jeans and a snugly fit dark-green T-shirt. That shirt is highlighting every rippling muscle in his chest and stomach. Is Rosie out of her dang gone mind? And she said he can hold it down in the sack, too? As she can say—oh hell no! I notice that Alejandro has gotten the attention of quite a few of the ladies—Odell included. He sees me and walks over to where I'm sitting.

"Hi there, beautiful," he says as he bends down and gives me a little kiss on the lips.

"*Hola*. I'm glad you decided to come. I knew you would."

"Yeah, I didn't want Rhonda to be mad at me."

"I made your favorite dish—*chuletas de puerco*. Just in case they were eaten all up, I put aside some for you in the stove."

"Thanks, Nikki." He gives me another quick peck on the lips. "You're such a sweetheart."

Mario clears his throat. I turn my head and see him looking directly at me. Right now his eyes are green, more from envy than color.

"Oh, Alejandro, this is Mario, our friend who moved out to L.A. Mario, this is Alejandro."

"What's up, man? Nice to meet you."

"Same here."

They reach across me and shake hands.

"L.A., huh? Both my sister and my brother moved out to Hermosa Beach and have been trying to get me out there for the longest. I might go ahead and do it one of these days."

"Really? Don't be too hasty, my man. Cali ain't for everybody." Mario's tone was polite, but I caught the undercurrents of it, which weren't all that friendly.

"Um, Mario, Alejandro and Rosie have been dating and I'm hoping that she'll make him a member of the family one day."

Mario looks at me and I can see the relief in his face.

"Oh, you and Rosie are dating?" he asks Alejandro.

"We had been. Not that much lately." He shrugs his shoulders nonchalantly, but his feelings are anything but detached.

As if on cue, Rosie walks over to us.

"Hi, stranger," she says to Alejandro.

"Hello, Rosie."

He stands up and gives her a long, warm hug. She slips her arm under his.

"I'm going to steal him from you all a minute," she says to Mario and me. "Come on. Let's put your gift up and get some food in that belly."

I look at them as they walk off. They make such a great couple. *Wake up, Rosie.*

I glance back to Mario and blush. "You thought he was one of my suitors, didn't you?"

"What are you talking about?"

"You were so jealous. I could tell."

He grins. "No, I wasn't."

"Cali ain't for everybody, my man," I say mockingly.

"I wasn't jealous."

"Mmm-hmm." I lean over and give him a kiss. "Now when you're finished with your plate, I want you to make me some margaritas."

"Definitely. That'll come in handy when I want to take advantage of you later."

"Please, you could make Kool-Aid and still take advantage of me."

"Is that right?" he says, nibbling on my ear.

"Stop that!"

"Why?" he says, giving me an impish look.

"You know that my ears and neck are my hot spots."

"Oh, your neck, too? How could I forget about that?" He goes for my neck.

I shrink back, giggling.

"May I have your attention, everyone?!" Crystal shouts. "It's time for the mother-to-be and the father-to-be to open the gifts."

Alejandro puts two chairs beside the gift table, and Rhonda and Dante walk over and sit down. They take turns opening the gifts as Crystal and Odell pass them down. Rosie's videotaping and Chico's snapping pictures. They end up with two strollers, a bassinet, four diaper bags, clothes, gift certificates for diapers and formula, at least fifteen bottles, baby tubs, toys... Let's just say Rhonda could drop triplets and still would have more than enough.

CHAPTER SIX / *Seis*

Mario's stuck with bartending duties for a while. You know how folks are. Once they see someone with something, they want it also, which is what happened when people saw Chico and me sipping on margaritas that Mario made. Even though we've got beer, wine, wine coolers, Jack Daniel's, Jim Beam, Vox, and Hennessy out and available—that's not enough; they want margaritas also. So right now Mario's blowing up the blender.

Alejandro, Dante, Chico and a couple other guys are at one of the tables playing Dominoes, while a few other men are at another table playing cards. Other people are milling about socializing or dancing to "I Get Around" by Tupac. Rosie, Rhonda, Crystal, Odell, and I are sitting together at a table.

I notice a new arrival coming late. It's Thomas, our neighbor Sabrina's new boyfriend. Ugly must be taking a holiday. We've already got damn near a yard full of fine brothers and here comes another. Sabrina started dating Thomas recently and is already head over heels in love. I ain't mad at her. Thomas is a fine, tall glass of water that you want to sip slowly. He looks like a darker-skinned version of Boris Kodjoe. Not to slight my baby Mario and Alejandro, who have awesome bodies. Compared to Thomas' sculpted frame, he makes them seem like they go to the gym to look at the weights instead of lift them. Oh my.

"Here comes our crush, Rosie," I say.

She turns her head to look and she breaks out into a big grin.

"Oh, hell yeah! He knows he fine, girl."

"He's hot," Rhonda says in an awed tone.

"He sure is," says Crystal, leaning forward. "Who is that?"

"That's Thomas. Sabrina's man," answers Rosie.

"Wha-ah. Hold up! Put the tape on pause!" Odell says, holding up his hand. "That's the new boyfriend y'all was talkin' about Sabrina had?"

"Yeah," I say. "Why?"

Odell purses his lips and cuts his eyes upward.

"What, Odell?" asks Rosie. "You know him or something?"

Odell crosses his arms and legs and starts humming, still looking upward.

"No way!" I exclaim. "Do not tell me you *know* him."

Rosie snaps her fingers at Odell. "Okay, spill it, bitch."

"Should I spill it?" Odell asks to himself, putting a finger on his chin. "No. I think I'll save that tea and spill it some other time."

"You better start talking," says Rosie.

"Yeah, Odell," Rhonda says.

"Okay, y'all done pried it out of me." He scoots his chair closer to the table. "I met him summer 'fore last when he walked up in Menjo's."

We all lean in closer to listen.

"Chile, he had everybody's head turning like we was in *The Exorcist*. But me, being the fastest sissy of the west side, I made it to him first. I bought him some dranks and we got a little convo going. Now, at the time, he was living with some crow named Delores. He said he needed to have his breaks now and then to explore the other side. And honey, we ended up doing some explorin' later on that night. Just a little explorin', mind you. Odell don't put out all the good china the first night. After that we hooked up wherever, whenever—at his house when nobody was home, mine when nobody was home, Rouge Park. We went strong for at least two months or so. Then I started falling in love." Looking upward, he raises his hand and makes a falling gesture. "Falling like a star from a moonlit sky."

"Oh, brother," we all grumble.

"This bitch is so dramatic," says Rosie.

"A-ny-way," he says, rolling his eyes and smacking his lips. "One night I told him how I felt and that I wanted to only be with him. Shoot, I was fixin' to leave Roberta and *everythang*. But you know that Negro had the nerve to say 'I can't be in no relationship with another man.'"

"What?" Rhonda says incredulously. "No he didn't."

"Oh yes, he did, girl. Here we is laying up there in bed naked as jaybirds and he gonna say he can't be in no relationship with a man. We'd been sneakin' on dates like dinner and the movies. Hell, technically we was already in a relationship. I wanted it to be open and exclusive. Any-who, I broke it off after that; I knew how that story was gonna end—Odell, broken-hearted."

"We shouldn't be surprised, I guess," I say. "These days so many people are up for any and everything." I cut my eyes to Rhonda and we exchange knowing looks.

We all look over at Thomas, who's standing behind Sabrina with his arms wrapped around her. They seem like the picture-perfect couple.

"Do you think someone should tell Sabrina?" I ask.

"No," says Rosie. "You know how she is. If you try and tell her anything about some man she's seeing, she automatically thinks you're lying and you're jealous of her. You remember how you tried to tell her when you found out that guy Clarence was married?"

I nod my head.

"She told you to stay out of her business and that you were hating on her— knowing damn well that you're not like that."

"Really?" asks Odell. "Oh, she wrong for that. If it ain't coming from some-body that be all in folks' business and be causing trouble, you need to listen."

"I know," says Rosie. "And what ended up happening? She ran into him, his wife and their two kids downtown at the African Festival. And that time Zoe tried to tell her that that other dude was a crack dealer. Sabrina said the same shit to her. It had to take him getting busted by the police for her to believe it. She's one of those females that you can't warn that the stove is hot; they gotta get burned themselves. If we tell her anything, she's not going to listen. So when she walks in on him with his dick up some man's ass—she'll find out."

"Uh-uh!" Crystal exclaims.

Odell, Rhonda, and I chuckle.

"You know," Odell says, running a hand across his cornrows. "I think I'll go over to Miss Sabrina and have her introduce me to her new man."

"Odell, you wouldn't!" I say.

"Wouldn't I?" he says, smiling at me. "Trick, you know me. I ain't scared to stir up some shit every now and then."

"Weren't you just talking about folks being in other folks' business and causing trouble?" Rosie asks.

Odell tilts his head like he's thinking for a moment. "Yes, I did say that, didn't I?"

He gets up and sashays over to where Sabrina and Thomas are standing. All of us are looking on with our mouths agape. The expression that comes over Thomas' face when he sees Odell is priceless. If no one thinks black folks can go pale, Thomas is exhibit A.

Rhonda's amused. "I can't believe he's doing that."

"Me neither," Crystal says. "I wish we could hear what they're saying."

"He's a trip," Rosie says.

A few minutes later, Odell walks back to the table. Sabrina seems fine, but Thomas looks like he's praying for the ground to open and swallow him.

"What did you say, Odell?" all of us are asking at the same time.

"Calm down, hens. I did what I said I was gonna do. Soon as he saw me, he looked like a turd was about to fall down his pants leg and on the grass. After she introduced us, I said, 'Don't I know you from somewhere?' He was stuttering, 'No, no I don't think so.' I said, 'You sure? 'Cause you look awfully familiar.' Then I dropped it and chitchatted a bit—enjoying every bead of sweat I was putting on his fo'head."

"You are terrible," I say.

"I ain't thinkin' 'bout that on-the-downlow bastard. I'ma leave him alone. I'm here to have a good time."

The song "One More Chance" by Biggie Smalls comes on.

"That's my song!" Odell starts dancing and snapping his fingers. "I'll see y'all later. I'ma dance my ass on over to where that cutie is sitting by the stereo."

I decide to get up and groove, too. After dancing a little bit, I notice Odell tying to get his new friend to get up and join him. He's smiling and shaking his head. I go over to where they are.

"Come on and dance with us," I tell the guy. I take him by the hand and we start dancing, with me in the middle facing Odell.

"Hey!" Odell shouts. "Go, Nikki! It's yo' birthday!"

I then turn to face the other guy to dance. Odell's moving up on my backside with his hands on my hips. I turn again to Odell and put my arms on his shoulders.

Maybe it's the drinks I've had, but I'd swear Odell has a hard-on. Dang, my second one today. But I shouldn't be so quick to take credit for that, since his new friend's probably exciting him. I dance a little more, then I slip out of the middle. I look at Odell and the guy and wave. They wave and continue to dance. I walk back to the table and sit down.

"Y'all were getting a little down and dirty out there," Crystal teases.

"Yeah, it was a little menagerie going on," Rosie chimes in. "Speaking of which, I haven't had one of those in a while."

"Not in front of the little one's ears." Rhonda holds her stomach.

"How many times have you done a ménage a trois?" asks Crystal.

"Only five."

"Only five?" Rhonda and I ask in unison.

"Shit, I could've been in more than that. I don't know what y'all talking about."

"Did you like it?" Crystal asks.

"Uh, derr," I say. "She must like it, if she's done it five times."

Crystal smiles. "Forget you, Nikki."

"Yeah, I dig it. Contrary to how it may sound, I don't do it that often. Just every once in a while when I want to have some added spice in the boudoir. Alejandro said he wouldn't mind trying it; just not with another man. Have you ever done that, Crys?"

"Naw, girl. Uh-uh."

It's something about the way she says that that makes me not believe her. I glance over to Rhonda and our eyes meet. I can tell she's not buying it either.

"Maybe I can initiate you and Alejandro." Rosie says it in a teasing manner, but she's serious.

"No thank you, Rosie. That's okay," Crystal says, holding up her hand.

Right then Mario comes out of the house carrying a pitcher of margaritas. He gets a chair from another table and sits down between Rhonda and me.

"Last pitcher, everybody. We finally ran out of margarita mix and please, don't anyone go to the store to get any more."

All of us except Rhonda get our glasses ready to be filled. I'm already good and buzzed from the other two glasses that I had, along with the Negra Modelo and a shot of Vox.

Rhonda pouts. "I hate I have to miss out on your margaritas."

Mario puts his arm around her and she puts her head on his shoulder.

"Aww, I'm sorry," he says. "I'm coming back home for a few days at Christmastime. I'll be sure to mix up a special batch just for you."

"I'm gonna hold you to that. Your niece will be practically crawling by then."

"I can't wait to see her," he says. "I'll manage to spoil her all the way from California. Be sure to send me pictures right when you take them. As soon as Nikki told me you were having a girl, I said, 'Oh no, she'll probably be like you, Nikki and Rosie. Running the neighborhood, wreaking havoc on the block.'"

"All right now. We weren't that bad, were we?" Rhonda asks.

"Yes," Rosie says, chuckling.

"By the time I got to know you guys," Crystal says, "you'd calmed down. I heard of the scuffles you'd gotten into. But I only remember one fight you all were in."

"Oh yeah," I say. "When those sisters who transferred from Cooley High were talking mess to us. Calling me and Rosie Spics and Rhonda white trash. They were talking plenty of shit when they had an audience, but I bet they didn't say anything when we cornered their asses in the bathroom."

"Now that was worth getting suspended for," says Rosie.

"Really," I say. "Nobody else even thought to say anything to us after that, once they saw we could beat up some girls from Cooley—as rough as that school is."

"What are y'all over here gabbing about?" Chico asks, bringing a chair to sit down.

"About how Rosie, Nikki, and Rhonda used to be bullies," says Mario. "And how," he adds, patting Rhonda's belly, "this one might end up continuing the legacy."

"In all fairness," I say, "we weren't bullies. Bullies go around picking on people and beating them up for no reason. We always had just cause to dish out an ass whipping."

Rhonda giggles. "For real!"

Rosie states, "Like that time Nik and I had to get in Chico's ass."

"Aw, man, here we go." Chico grins and throws his hands up. "For the gazillionth time, I let y'all get at me 'cause I didn't believe in hitting on girls."

"Yeah right!" Rosie and I say.

Mario slaps him gently on the back. "I can't even buy that, bro."

"Thanks a lot, man."

"From what I recall, when Dad and I got home, Mom said you came in the house with a bloody nose saying that some boys had jumped you."

We all chuckle.

"Boys?" Rosie asks.

"What?" I say. "You never told me he said that!"

"Yeah. Dad was so upset that he put Chico in the car and drove around for him to point them out. Dad wanted to, as he said, 'Give these boys a good talking to.'"

Rhonda holds onto her belly. "Stop with the funny shit. You're gonna make me go into labor."

Chico gets up and goes behind Mario and gives him a playful choke. "Why you gotta have such a big mouth, dawg? Huh?"

"Okay, man. I'm sorry, I'm sorry."

Chico goes back and sits down.

"You'd kept your mouth closed all these years, why you yapping now? I'll really never hear the end of it. Shit, truth be told, I felt like I'd been beat up by a couple of boys. I couldn't believe that two girls, much less girls that looked like y'all, could throw down like that."

"NYC, big boy-yee!" Rosie shouts.

"Yay e yay-eee!" I shout.

Rosie and I stand up and double high-five each other across the table.

Mario, Chico, Rhonda, and Crystal are laughing and staring at us like we're crazy.

"Okay," Mario says as he slides my margarita glass from me. "You're officially cut off. Chico, grab Rosie's glass, too, man."

I pick up my glass. "I'm barely getting started."

"One time I came close to kicking Rosie's ass," Rhonda says.

"Me? When?" Rosie asks.

"When you fucked up my hair that time, that's when."

We all burst into laughter.

"Y'all still remember that shit, huh? I was so upset I cried and cried. Y'all cousin Enrique and I had been talking on the phone right before he came to stay for the summer and I really liked him and wanted to look good for him. I begged Daddy for money to get new outfits and everything. Enrique said he liked girls with curly hair so I was going to get my hair like that. But instead of following my first mind and getting my hair professionally permed, I let this heifer here talk me into letting her do it. I'm expecting my hair to be curly like Nikki's but instead I ended up looking like Little Orphan Annie."

"It's a hard knock life for us," I sing. Chico and Rosie join me. "It's a hard life for us."

"Forget y'all!" Rhonda continues. "I had to wear a hat when he got here."

"You wore that hat for almost the entire summer," Mario adds.

"I know. Every time I looked in the mirror, I wanted to choke Rosie."

"I almost got beat down for that, huh?" Rosie giggles.

"Yeah, you almost got beat all the way down."

"I followed the instructions on the box. I don't know what happened."

"I knew something had gone wrong when I looked at Nikki, after you took out the curler rods. Her eyes were as big as saucers. She had this 'oh my God' look on her face."

"One of my boys saw you when you were over Nikki and Rosie's house without your hat," says Chico. "He was like, 'Yo, who's the white chick with the 'fro?' You looked like a white Foxy Brown and shit."

We all snicker.

After the amusement dies down, I lift my glass. "All right, everybody, lift your glasses."

I go to the next table and get a pitcher of lemonade and pour Rhonda a glass.

"I want to give a toast to..." I take a sip of my drink. "I want to give a toast first to Rhonda—the first of us to be blessed with bringing a new generation of hell raisers into the family. *Salud!*"

"*Salud!*" everyone says.

"Secondly, I want to give a toast to Mario. This is to him landing a full-time writing gig at *Urban Report* magazine back in L.A."

"What?" Rhonda exclaims. She puts her glass down and gives Mario a big hug.

"That's great!" Crystal says. "I'm happy for you, Mario."

"Me, too," Rosie agrees. She gets up and gives him a hug also.

Chico shakes his hand. "Congrats, bro!"

"Thanks, everybody," Mario says.

Crystal gets up to give him a hug and plants a kiss on his lips. The kiss lasts a couple of seconds too long for my liking. My eyes don't leave her until she's back in her seat.

"Mario," I say. "I'll be giving you some more congratulations later on tonight."

"Nikki!" Rhonda exclaims.

Rosie's giggling and clapping her hands.

"All righty then," Chico states with a chuckle.

"Can I get that in writing?" Mario asks, smiling.

"You can get it any way you want to."

"Damn!" exclaims Rosie. She and Crystal high-five each other.

Chico looks at me. "Nikki, you gots to be toasted."

"I ain't feeling no pain; that's for sure." I pour the last of the margarita into my glass.

"Hey now," Mario says, "if you keep drinking like that, you won't be able to finish congratulating me later."

"Please, I can drink all y'all under the table."

"You're right, Chico," Rosie says. "She's toasted. You can tell when she starts talking shit."

"Look, I'm a bit tipsy, but I got all my facoo... facil... faculties."

Everyone laughs. I sit down.

"Like I said," Rosie states sarcastically.

"Ohh! Guess who I saw the other day, y'all?" asks Rhonda.

"Who?" we ask.

"Jasmine," she answers, looking at Chico.

We break out laughing.

"We used to call her 'The Jasmanian Devil,'" I say.

"I remember," Rosie says. "That child was hit–to' up from the flo' up. But Chico was in love with her."

"I wasn't in love with her. I was in love with her poon-tang."

"No he didn't just say 'poon-tang,'" Rosie comments. "Nigga, just say pussy. I ain't heard poon-tang since second grade."

"All right then," Chico says. "Pussy. She had some good pussy."

"The fellas used to call her butter face," says Mario. "'Cause everything about her looked good..."

"But her face!" we all finish.

"What can I say, ma put it on me," says Chico. "Did you speak to her, Rhonda? Or did you just see her?"

"I only saw her. She was in line ahead of me at Kroger's. She had a baby on her hip."

"Ohh!" says Rosie. "How old did the baby look?"

"Like he was about two years old."

"Whew!" Chico says. "It ain't mine then, thank goodness."

"How did the baby look? Like her?" I ask.

"No comment. You know how when you talk about other people's kids, it comes back on you. So I ain't trying jinx little Jada."

"Jada?" Rosie asks. "That's what you're naming her?"

"Yeah, Dante and I finally settled on that name last night."

"Aww," I say. "That's a pretty name. Little Jada Pinkett-Smith."

Rhonda giggles. "At first I wanted to name her Mariah, but Dante said it reminded him of pariah. I ignored him at first, then I couldn't think of that name without thinking pariah."

"I like the name Jada, too," says Crystal.

"Uh-oh, she more like little Chita Rivera the way she's doing these high kicks. Calm down in there," Rhonda says to her belly.

"Can I feel?" asks Mario.

"Of course."

Mario puts his hand on her belly and his face lights up.

"Wow! That is amazing."

"I want to feel her," Rosie says. She gets up and goes to Rhonda. She puts her hand on her belly.

"She's ready to come out of there, girl."

"It's probably all the music and me giggling so much."

After that, Chico, Crystal and I take turns feeling Jada kick.

"Hey, my turn."

I swing around and see Alejandro, standing there smiling.

"Get on over here, hon," says Rhonda, smiling.

Alejandro goes over to feel the baby kick.

"I guess she doesn't like me." He grins. "She stopped kicking."

"Aw, I'm sorry," says Rhonda. "You'll catch her next time."

"Okay." He kisses Rhonda on the forehead and then gets a chair to sit next to Rosie.

"It doesn't get on your nerves, all of us hovering to feel your belly?" I ask.

"No, chile. It's only when people I don't know want to come up and do it. I was in Walgreen's one day and this woman who I didn't know from Adam, came up on me and put her hand on my stomach. I'm like, no you didn't. I mean, she didn't ask or nothing. I wanted to pop the shit out of her so bad."

"I know you did," says Crystal.

"But you know y'all are different."

"That girl's definitely going to be spoiled," I say. "Look at all the attention she's getting and she's not even born yet."

"Really," says Rhonda. "Plus her daddy's always talking to her. You should see how she responds to his voice. I swear she starts dancing. We're talking a straight-up daddy's girl."

Rhonda has the look of pure joy lighting up her face. It tugs at my heart to see my friend so happy. I kind of feel a bit guilty because, when she first told me she was pregnant, my first thought was, "Oh no, now she's bringing a baby into the mess of Dante's gambling problem." Rhonda was slightly hesitant at first. But now she wants nothing more than to have this baby. And despite how I feel about Dante, I'm so looking forward to Jada's entrance into our crazy family.

CHAPTER SEVEN / *Siete*

The baby shower has started to wind down. It would've gone on longer, but most of the guests have left to go to a birthday party being thrown at the Comfort Zone by our friend Zoe. Rosie, Crystal, Odell, and I are clearing the food table and the discarded gift paper. Mario has borrowed Chico's car to go see their parents. I notice Rhonda walking toward us.

"All right, everybody. This youngun' and I are tired as hell. I'm gonna go on home and haul all this ass into bed."

"I wish you didn't have to go, but you're beat."

"Nik, you don't know the half of it. You all going to Zoe's party?"

"No," answers Rosie. "We're gonna stay here and chill. Light up a little indo." Rhonda wrinkles up her nose.

"Yeah," Rosie adds. "You ain't done that since that last time when you started *noiding*."

"Somebody knocked at the door," I say. "And you were like, 'Ah! Ah! It's the police! It's the police!' And your ass ran into the bathroom and flushed a perfectly good joint down the toilet. We were so mad at you."

We all chuckle.

"And then," Rosie adds, "you started spraying air freshener like crazy and crying at the same time that you didn't want to go to jail and you wanted your mommy."

"Forget y'all." Rhonda waves us off. "I wasn't doing all that."

"Yes, you were," Rosie says.

"Whatever, I guess that was my 'just say no' moment. Whew! I'm so full from all that food. Everything was delicious. Well, almost everything. Surely, neither one of you made those greens. So who was the culprit?"

"Girl," I say, "It was Jeannette with her non-cooking ass. Why we didn't make some back-up greens when she said that's what she was bringing, I don't know. Weren't they pitiful?"

"They were like rubber," says Crystal.

"Ain't had no taste to 'em," adds Odell. "I coulda took some tree leaves, threw it in the pot wit' some Lawry's and a ham hock and came out the kitchen wit' somethin' betta than that."

"I know that's right," Rhonda and I say together.

"Did you see old ass Miss Beverly all dancin' up on them young bucks?" asks Odell.

Rhonda exclaims, "I was cracking up!"

"Her horny ass. She lookin' for somebody to knock the wrinkles and dust out that ole twat."

Rosie shakes her head. "Odell, you crazy!"

"And my goodness," says Odell. "That daughter of hers. I'ma have to find the time to become her friend. She need a fag like me in her life to teach her how to dress. She know she need a good butt whuppin', wearing that there Moms Mabley dress."

We all crack up.

"She a young girl. I don't why she dress so frumpy. Here she is in her twenties and be dressin' in them mother of the bride type of clothes. The mother of the bride that married late in life at that."

I tell him, "You're wrong for that, Odell."

"She talkin' 'bout she lookin' fo' a man," he continues. "Ain't no man gone be lookin' for her if she don't get a Jenny Jones makeover. Shit, Jenny Jones, Ricki Lake, Maury Povich, and Oprah. Everybody need to pitch in and help that child. I was talkin' to her and I was tellin' her that she'd look nicer, you know, if she put on a little makeup. I told her what color lipstick would look good on her. Hell, you see what Avon did for them Williams sisters. She gone talk about, 'My mama said I don't need no makeup.' I said, 'Humph! The same way yo' mama lied to you about Santa, the Tooth Fairy and the Easter Bunny, she lyin' to you 'bout that, too.' I shut that noise real quick."

"Odell…" My eyes have started to tear up. "That wasn't nice."

Rhonda has an arm around Rosie's shoulder and is leaning on her, also in tears. Crystal's laughing, but it doesn't look like she quite knows what she's laughing at. She's lit. She's been going with me drink for drink. But I can handle mine. Pretty much.

"The truth ain't always nice," says Odell. "It's rare that Odell can hold her tongue. Look like her mama shoulda done told her somethin', 'stead of lying to the poor chile. Then again her mama need help herself with that skunk tail she had throwed up on her head. Lookin' like somethin' she bought on clearance from the Della Reese Collection."

"Odell…" Rosie bends over and grabs her stomach. "You need to quit!"

Odell clears his throat and then whispers, "Miss Rosie, you need to start. I see Alejandra still lurking about. You better go on and give that boy a piece. I would, if he was lookin' for a job in my field."

"Really," says Crystal. "He is delicious. I wouldn't mind some of that."

"Okay," says Rosie. "I thought you were buzzing, but now I know."

"Mmm-hmm," Crystal says as she sways to the song "The Way" by Jill Scott.

Rhonda mimics Crystal's dance motion. "Look at this hot cocked heifer. Talking 'bout some "mmm-hmm."

Rosie, Odell, and I snicker.

Dante walks up to us. He stands behind Rhonda with his arms around her, his hands resting on her belly. He almost can make me forget that I can't stand his ass and that I only tolerate him for Rhonda's sake.

"Everything's in the truck, baby," he says. "Except for the strollers. Junior's going to take them in his car."

"Okay, baby." Rhonda turns to Rosie and motions for the rest of us to come over. "Group hug time."

We all gather around to embrace her.

"Thanks so much for doing this for me. It was so wonderful. I really do appreciate it." Tears are misting her eyes.

"Don't start that," Rosie playfully admonishes. "No waterworks. You better save those tears for the delivery room."

"You ain't lying. I'd better."

Rosie kisses her on the cheek, so do Odell, Crystal and me.

I reach for two big plates of food that I prepared and wrapped for her.

"Here you go, Rhonda. This is for you and Dante. Especially you; you get those cravings in the middle of the night. Don't worry; I didn't put any of those greens in there."

"Thank goodness." She gives me a long hug. "I love you, girl."

"And I love you."

"I'll see you guys; probably in the next day or so. Nikki, I'll call you tomorrow and we'll get together on a day and time so we can get the thank you cards sent out."

"Okay, sweetie. That sounds good."

"I want to thank y'all also," says Dante. "This was real cool and we appreciate it. I wish that my family could've made it in from Alabama. They would've enjoyed it."

"You're welcome, Dante," I say.

"We were more than happy to do it," Rosie responds. She says this through a clenched, fake smile. She likes Dante even less than I do.

"Anytime, dahlin'." Odell offers with a flirtatious grin. Now, I've had a couple of surprises today, but he's definitely barking up the wrong tree now.

"Bye," Rhonda says.

"Bye!"

She and Dante leave the backyard. He's carrying the plates, one on top of the other with one hand, and has his other arm around her waist.

"I don't know why y'alls don't like Dante," Odell says.

"'Cause, Rhonda deserves better," I say.

"Really," says Rosie. "It's hard enough to raise a baby, but it's gonna be harder with his ass going around hocking everything to gamble."

"You can tell how much he love her though," Odell says.

"Ain't nobody trying to hear that," Rosie says.

"So, his love don't count for nothing?"

"No!" we both say.

"Y'all some stubborn ole crones. What you think, Crystal?"

"Huh?" she says.

"Crystal's enjoying her buzz," Rosie informs us. "She ain't thinking about what we're talking about."

"Oh, shit," I say as I feel raindrops. "Let's hurry and get this stuff inside."

We start gathering up the dishes and taking them in the house. Alejandro and Chico, who were in front talking to Chico's boys before they left, are getting the stereo equipment together to take inside. Soon the rain starts falling even harder.

"We can leave the decorations and stuff out until tomorrow," I tell everyone. "And the tables and chairs are weatherproof so we won't worry about them."

We all rush into the house. Odell and I put up the leftovers and pots and pans in the dishwasher. Alejandro, Rosie and Crystal are in the living room talking. When Odell and I are finished, we join them.

"Where's Chico?" I ask.

"He's upstairs," answers Rosie. "I think he's taking a shower."

"Well, I guess I'll see y'all. Odell 'bout to get on home."

"Bitch, who you think you fooling?" Rosie asks sarcastically.

"What, Miss Rosie?"

"Don't 'what, Miss Rosie' me. Your ass ain't going nowhere near home. On a Saturday night and it ain't even eleven o'clock yet?" She sucks her teeth. "Please."

Odell looks at her, smiling. "Okay, well I might make a little stop somewheres."

"See, I know you!"

"You sho do." He goes over and kisses her and Crystal on the cheek.

"Bye now, Alejandra."

"Yeah, later, Odell."

"I'll walk you to the front door."

"Okay, Nikki."

"Careful out there!" shouts Rosie.

"You know it, *mamacita.*"

When I open the front door, rain is pouring down.

"Odell, you sure you don't wanna stay put for a bit? It's crazy raining."

"No, I can make it."

"Anxious to get to Jamal, huh?" I inquire.

"Yes, chile. I ain't going to let a little rain get in between me and some..."

"Okay, okay. I get the picture."

I put my arms around his neck and give him a hug.

"You be careful."

"I will."

He pulls back a little with his arms still around my waist.

"I better get on outta here 'fore you put wood in my panties again."

I'm shocked. "I did that? I noticed that you'd gotten, ahem, aroused earlier. But I thought it was your little friend who was getting to you."

"Uh-uh, it was you. Now, don't get me wrong. I ain't trying to suit up for the other team. You ain't converted Odell or nothing. It was jus' a li'l fly by night thang. Every once in a while you get a little hot fo' somebody that don't normally catch yo' eye. Don't mean you any different; you just can't help it sometimes. Once in a blue moon a cat might wanna see what a bone taste like and a dog may wanna try some milk. Don't mean the cat tryin' to be a dog and the dog tryin' to be a cat."

I stare at him for a minute. "What the hell are you talking about?"

"Chile, I don't know." He reaches in his pocket for his keys.

"Maybe you should reconsider going out driving, 'cause obviously you've had one too many."

"Please. Odell done made it from all the way over on the East Side, higher than this. I sho as hell can make it a few blocks." He opens the screen door. "Tell your cousin to call me when she wants me to snip them ends."

"All right, crazy. I'll have your casserole dish ready for you to pick up next time you're over."

"Okay. See ya."

"See you."

He runs to his car. I watch him as he drives off. I close the door and head back to the living room. As I reenter the room, I slightly lose my balance.

"Uh-huh. All them margaritas got to your ass," Rosie says.

"Oh shut up." I walk over to the stereo and look through the CDs.

"Play some old school salsa," Rosie says. "Ismael Rivera or Willie Colón or something."

I put on a CD by Ismael. I program it so that Bob Marley and Earth, Wind, and Fire play after that.

I go and sit on the couch. Rosie, Crystal and Alejandro are sitting on the opposite couch, with Rosie in the middle. How ironic—in an Alanis Morissette sense of ironic way.

"How many CDs did you put in?" Rosie asks.

"Three."

"It took you that long to program three CDs?" She laughs, as does Alejandro. Crystal grins and sips from her glass.

"I ain't thinking about y'all."

Chico comes downstairs dressed in a different outfit.

"Where are you going?" I ask.

"Brenda's coming over to pick me up."

"Her crazy ass ex-boyfriend ain't still coming around trying to cause trouble, is he?" Rosie asks.

"Naw, that fool finally took the hint."

"You be sure to keep an eye out for his ass. Thank goodness you saw him creeping in the bushes that time. Ain't no telling what he was up to."

"Trust me. Even though he hasn't made any move lately, I'm still cautious."

"That's good," I say.

"I'll be back," Rosie says as she gets up and heads upstairs.

I get up to go into the kitchen. "Anybody want anything?"

"Yeah, I'll have another Heineken, if any's left," Chico says.

"Any more Vox?" asks Alejandro.

"Yeah, I have another bottle. You want it straight or with juice?"

"Some cranberry juice, if you have any."

"Sure."

"Thanks."

"I'll have the same thing," Crystal says.

"All right."

When I get back to the living room with the drinks on a tray, Chico's on his cell phone. Alejandro and Crystal are sitting a lot closer than when I left the room. I place the tray on the cocktail table and hand everyone their drinks. Rosie comes back downstairs with a big blunt.

"What the fuck is that?" Chico asks. "A Cheech and Chong special?"

"Hell yeah." Rosie takes a hit, then sits back down on the couch. Crystal has to move a little so Rosie can reclaim her spot. She takes another hit and offers it to Alejandro; he shakes his head. She offers it to Crystal, who takes it and hits it two times. She leans forward and passes it to me. I take two tokes, cough and then hit it again.

"Puff, puff, pass," Chico says as he gets off his phone.

I pass it to him. He takes about four hits.

"You've got your damn nerve," I say.

By the time I get to my second round of toking, I feel...I feel...nice as hell. It feels like my body's floating inside my skin. I lie back against the sofa, sinking into the cushions. I hear Rosie offer me some more, but I decline. Considering what I've had to drink today, any more for me at this point would be overkill. I close my eyes and take note of every wave coursing throughout my body. I hear a car horn honking somewhere in the distance.

"I'll see y'all some time tomorrow," Chico says. "Rosie, that shit is tight. Save me a couple of hits."

"No problem. We ain't gonna smoke this whole big ass blunt."

"Nikki's knocked the fuck out." I feel him kiss me on the forehead.

"Take care, man," Alejandro says.

I feel myself fade out. I'm hearing that song by War in my head, "Slipping Into Darkness." How fucking appropriate.

I'm in PR visiting *abuela*. Rosie and I have just woken up and we're lying in bed planning what we're going to do for the day. We have to do as much as we can in these next two weeks before we go back home and back to school. I hear a bell ringing. It's Mr. Villanueva. He rolls his cart through the streets every morning except Sunday, selling his delicious, fresh-baked *mallorca*.

"*Mallorca! Mall-ooooorcaaaa!*" he shouts.

"Rosie! Go get some money from *abuela!* Hurry!"

"I'm hurrying."

"*Mallorca!*"

I put on my bunny slippers and run outside to meet Mr. Villanueva as he gets to our house. When I open the door, I'm back home. Rhonda's sitting at a gigantic table opening gifts.

"Hey, girl. This is the best baby shower ever. Have Mario make me a margarita."

"No, Rhonda. You know you're pregnant. I'll give you some *mallorca.*"

"Girl, she don't want none of that! Give her some of my banana pudding."

"Oh, hey, Odell. Yeah, I'll give her some of that."

"Chile, it's that best banana pudding in the world. Didn't I throw down on it, Nikki?"

"Uh-huh." Chico's starting his bike. "Where you going, Chico?"

"Somewhere quiet. Rosie makes too much noise. You hear that?"

I stop and listen. I can hear her. Chico's right; she is loud. I turn to go back into the house to tell her to keep it down. Jaime's standing at the back door with a shovel in his hand.

"Jaime, what are you doing here?"

He doesn't say anything. I take a step forward and fall into a deep hole in the ground. I awaken with a start.

When I open my eyes, the only light on is the one in the aquarium. I blink a few times to adjust my eyes. Across from me on the other couch, Rosie and Crystal are on either side of Alejandro. He has his shirt off. He and Rosie are kissing. He unties her halter top, takes it off, and throws it to the other side of the couch. He bends his head down and takes one of her breasts into his mouth. Crystal's on the couch on her knees behind him, stroking his dick through his pants and kissing the back of his neck. He lifts his head from Rosie's breast, takes his arm and puts it on the back of Crystal's head and they kiss. Rosie stands up and slips off her jeans and panties. Crystal stops kissing Alejandro and reaches to untie and take off her halter top and sits on the couch.

Rosie bends down and unbuckles Alejandro's belt and unzips his pants. He lifts his hips so that she can slide his pants and underwear off. Rosie sits down and starts to bend her head toward his dick. She puts it in her mouth and runs her tongue along the length of it. Crystal bends her head down, Rosie moves her head aside and Crystal takes Alejandro into her mouth and begins to suck him. She and Rosie take turns going down on him. Alejandro's leaning back onto the couch. His hips are gyrating and he's moaning. Each of his hands is stroking the hair of Rosie and Crystal. He looks like he's in a state of pure bliss.

Rosie and Crystal stop what they're doing and begin kissing each other. They begin fondling each other's breasts. I feel my eyelids get heavy and darkness overtakes me.

I open my eyes and see that Rosie, Crystal, and Alejandro are all naked. Rosie's on the couch and Crystal's on her knees going down on Rosie. Rosie's grabbing her head and loudly moaning. Alejandro's behind Crystal. He's putting on a condom. He then enters Crystal from behind. Crystal lifts her head momentarily to let out a cry of pleasure, then goes back to going down on Rosie.

Rosie's pulling Crystal's head deeper into her. Alejandro's furiously pumping away in Crystal, then suddenly he stops. Crystal lifts her head from Rosie and looks back at him.

"Why did you stop?" she asks.

"I don't want to come yet, baby," he replies.

He pulls out of Crystal. She stands up.

"Come sit on the couch," she tells Alejandro.

He gets up and sits on the couch a few inches from Rosie. He leans over and gives Rosie a kiss. Crystal straddles him, lowering herself down onto him. He grabs her ass and his head moves to the side. He's sucking her breast. Crystal begins to gyrate her hips wildly. She wraps her arms around his shoulders and he holds her tightly around her waist. Soon, Crystal throws her head back and cries out. A few moments later Alejandro lets out a loud guttural groan. Their movements gradually slow down. Crystal takes Alejandro's head in her hands and gives him a lingering kiss.

My curiosity mixed with voyeurism wants to continue to see how this plays out, but as hard as I'm trying to fight it, the curtains close.

CHAPTER EIGHT / *Ocho*

I'm awakened by the sound of the doorbell. I look about and see that the living room is empty, save for myself. The pillows from the couch are strewn about and there are glasses on the table. I get up to answer the door. As I do, I fall back down on the couch. I raise up and head for the door. I look through the peephole and see that it's Mario. I open the door.

"Hey, Mario."

"Hey, yourself. It's about time you opened the door." He kisses me on the forehead and enters.

"Sorry. I guess I was sleeping it off. What time is it?"

Looking at his watch, he says, "It's a quarter to one. Where is everyone?"

We sit down on the couch.

"I don't know. Oh, Chico's over Brenda's house. I don't know where Rosie, Crystal, and Alejandro are."

"There's a red Expedition out front."

"That's Crystal's. Did you see Rosie's car in the driveway?"

"Yeah." He looks around the living room.

"Maybe they took the party upstairs."

"What the..." He leans forward, looking at something on the table. "What's a condom wrapper doing on the table?"

"That's Alejandro's, I guess."

"You guess? What the hell went on here? What do you mean, they took the party upstairs?"

"Baby, not so many questions at once."

Mario's face is set. He's looking at me intently, waiting for answers.

"Look, right before Chico left out, Rosie lit up a blunt and we all hit it; everyone except Alejandro anyway. That mixed with the drinks I had earlier had me floating to Never Land. When I woke up, Chico was gone and the three of them were going at it."

"Going at it? You mean having sex?"

"No, playing Three Card Monte."

"That was a dumb question." He blushes and nods at the wrapper. "That tells it all." He pauses, looking at me. "You didn't partake in the 'party,' did you?"

"No, baby. Shit, as much as I was weirdly fascinated by it all, I could barely keep my eyes open. They could've thrown the dang gone wrapper away, instead of leaving it on the table. I hope they didn't put any stains on the couch."

"You're sounding cranky." He chuckles, putting an arm around my waist.

"I can't believe what went down, or rather who went down. Alejandro was getting at Crystal and she was going down on Rosie."

"What? I assumed that Alejandro was getting his. I didn't think Crystal was down for getting it on with Rosie."

"I'm finding out that Crystal is down for pretty much anything. You ready for bed?"

"I'm ready for you."

"Same here. I'd kiss you but I've got blunt breath." I stand up. "I'm going to hop in the shower real quick."

He stands up also. "Can I take one with you?"

"Hmm, I guess." I take his hand and we head upstairs. I'm feeling a bit woozy, but I'll be fine once I hit the shower.

"Mom and Dad said to tell you and Rosie hi and they want us to come over for dinner next weekend."

"That sounds good. Did you tell your dad about your new job?"

"Yeah. He'd rather that I'd done like Chico and gone into the computer repair business with him. He wants nothing more than to change the name of the company from Esposito and Son to Esposito and Sons. But he's happy for me. Mom screamed louder than you did when I told her."

I pause by Rosie's door, tilting my head to listen.

"Nosy," Mario whispers.

I can hear moaning and the sound of the bed squeaking. I can't resist. I turn the door handle and quietly open the door. Rosie has her night table lamp on low and she's on top of Crystal, pumping away. She's holding down Crystal's hands with her own. There's a strap around Rosie's waist. I guess she has on her now infamous strap-on. Crystal seems to be enjoying that ten-inch piece of plastic. Alejandro is nowhere in sight. I slowly close the door. I turn to Mario. His mouth is hanging open. I lead him to my room and close the door.

"You're gonna catch a million flies with that open mouth."

"Crystal? You told me what happened earlier, but I guess seeing it is another thing. How long has this been going on with her and Rosie?"

"Tonight was the first and, hopefully, the last time."

"Why do you say that?"

"Rosie has feelings for Crystal, but for Crystal, it's only sex. Rhonda and I were talking about this earlier and I was telling her that I could see Rosie getting hurt from this."

"I thought Rosie was seeing Alejandro?"

"She was, but I think her feelings for Crystal always held her back from going to the next level with him. I only found out today from Rhonda that Crystal gets down like that."

"How did Rhonda know?"

"Dante's friend's brother is married to a chick Crystal was hanging with and the chick's husband caught them in bed together."

"Are you serious?"

"Shit!" I smack my forehead. "I forgot, Rhonda told me not to tell anybody."

"You know I'm not going to say anything."

"So did that scene you just saw excite you at all?" I tease.

"No, as a matter of fact it didn't. I think of Rosie and Crystal as sisters, more so Rosie. And seeing your sisters doing the do ain't exactly making a tent in my pants. That was weird as hell, seeing Rosie screwing her with that fake dick. That's not a good picture in my head."

I giggle and shake my head.

"What?"

"Rosie was playing with Chico earlier about having a strap-on, and he pretty much said the same thing about having that image in his head."

I put my arms around him and lightly kiss his neck. "I have to say, when I think about it, I got a little turned on by seeing Alejandro do his thing."

"Are you trying to deliberately tick me off, woman?"

"Um-hmm. And I'm trying to get you to rise to the challenge and get me even more turned on. But that'll have to wait for a bit." I abruptly pull away and walk toward my bathroom.

"Oh, you suck," he says.

"In due time, my dear."

I enter the bathroom and get my toothbrush from the holder.

"Let me go get mine," he says. He kisses me on the cheek. "I'll be right back."

"Okay."

By the time he returns, I've barely stepped into the shower.

"Hey, you were supposed to wait for me."

"Hurry up, hurry up."

A few moments later he pulls back the shower curtain suddenly. I jump.

"Grrr!" His mouth is full of toothpaste foam.

"You are stupid." I giggle.

He steps in and rinses his mouth off in the stream of water. We begin to lather each other all over, intermittently kissing. I soap my hands and take his hardened member and stroke it. His hand goes to my mound and his middle finger seeks and finds my clit. He strokes it gently. I pump my hips against his hand.

"Baby," I moan. "Let's finish this in the bedroom."

"Mmm. All right."

I turn the water off and we step out of the shower. We both take a towel from the towel rack and dry each other off. When we step into the bedroom, I go to my boom box and put in a mix tape of slow songs by the Isley Brothers. "Sensuality" is the first song that plays. I turn off the overhead light and turn on the torchiere lamp in the corner on low. Mario has lain down on the bed. I notice a package of condoms on the nightstand.

"Let me guess, you got those from the lady from Planned Parenthood."

He chuckles. "I can't believe you're still teasing me about that. Come here."

He reaches out his hand to me. I go to him, taking his hand in mine. He pulls me on top of him. I look down at him, staring into his eyes.

"I've missed you so much, Nik."

"I've missed you, too."

"It's been far too long, baby."

"It's funny. It's like we were just together yesterday."

"Mmm, yeah."

I kiss him long and deep. Then I slowly move my mouth down, intermingling kisses and licks, first to his neck and then his chest. I lick one nipple and lightly suck on it. I feel it harden beneath my tongue. Mario lets out a low moan. I move my mouth to his other nipple, licking it and ever so lightly running my teeth across it.

"Oh, Nikki, baby," he moans.

I lick his nipples a little more, then continue moving down his body, planting kisses on his stomach. I skip past his hard dick and lick his thighs, paying extra attention to the insides of them. When I do this, he squirms and groans with pleasure. I kiss on down to his calves and then make my ascent back up his body till I get to his dick. I can tell he's anticipating my mouth on it. I put my lips to it, breathing my warm breath on it. I lower my head to his balls. I take them in my mouth, softly sucking on them. I slip them out of my mouth, pressing my lips against them and running my tongue all over them—doing figure eights and short quick tongue flicks.

"Shit!" Mario says, breathing heavily.

I move up to his dick and, beginning at the shaft, I run my mouth along it to the head—pressing my tongue against the vein underneath it as I go. When I get to the head, I swirl my tongue around it. Mario's panting even harder and moving his hips. I take him into my mouth and move my head up and down, receiving as much of his nine inches that I can. I put my hand at the base of it, moving it up and down, keeping in time the motions of my mouth. I feel Mario signaling for me to stop. I look up at him.

"What is it, baby?"

"Turn around so I can do you, too," he says huskily.

I maneuver my body around and straddle his head. He spreads my lips, exposing my clit. When his tongue hits it, my body shivers from the wonderful sensation. I lightly grind down on his face. I put my mouth back on him and we pleasure each other for a few minutes. Every now and then Mario will make me stop when he's at the point of orgasm. Finally, I roll off him and gaze at him.

"I really need you inside of me right now."

I move to the top of the bed. Mario reaches over for the condoms. He opens one and puts it on. He slides between my welcoming legs. He bends his head and takes one of my breasts into his mouth, sucking and running his tongue across the nipple. Damn, it feels so good. He moves his head to the other breast and does the same. I pull his head up and kiss him passionately.

I reach down between us and guide him inside of me. He moves his hips in circles, giving me inch by delicious inch at a time. Soon he's completely inside of me. Our mouths haven't left one another. I grab his ass, feeling his movements. For a few strokes, he only enters me by a couple of inches, then plunges deep inside. He continues to do this, making me anticipate the next deep thrust. Our moans escape into each other's mouths. He breaks our kiss and moves his body up a couple of inches until his head is right above my head. His strokes are hitting right up against my clit.

"Shit, Nikki," he moans. "Oh, baby. Baby."

"Se siente tan bueno. Tan bueno."

Both of us are breathing laboriously. I feel the build-up as I move closer to orgasm. I slow my movement. I don't want to lose the spot on my clit that Mario is hitting. Soon, I reach my peak and my back stiffens, then arches slightly off the bed. I cry out, calling Mario's name. I feel almost as if I'm going to black out from the explosion within my body. I relax and my breathing starts to slow down. When Mario realizes my orgasm is over, he moves back down till we are face to face.

I speed back up the movement of my hips. I can tell that he's close to coming. His mouth is to my ear. The warmth of his breath on my earlobe is sending more tingling sensations throughout my body. He pumps his hips in rapid, circular strokes. I grab his firm, round ass and run my nails across it, igniting his nerve endings there. He grabs me tighter and raises his head. I look up at him and see the perspiration beading his forehead and the look of pleasure contorting his handsome face. He bites down on his bottom lip and then sharply intakes his breath, making a hissing noise. His mouth opens.

"Ahhhh shiiiiiiitttt!" he cries out as he orgasms.

He continues moving his hips a little for a few moments. His body finally relaxes. I stroke his backside lovingly. He showers my face with kisses. We gaze into each other's eyes.

"That was fucking incredible, baby," he says softly.

"Both literally and figuratively."

He chuckles. "You got that right. I'm going to be feeling that one for days. It was too damn good. I had to work like a mutha not to come too soon. I was thinking about baseball, 90-year-old ladies in thongs..."

I pull him to me. He kisses me on the lips and then grabs on to the top of the condom and pulls out of me. He rolls over on his back and I turn to the side and lay my head on his chest. He wraps his arm around my waist. We lie silent for a few minutes, stroking each other.

He clears his throat. "I have a question."

"What is it?"

"Is it better with me, or with Jaime?"

His question catches me completely off guard. I lift my head to look at him. He has such a vulnerable expression that I feel my heart swell.

"Baby, I won't lie to you. I enjoyed it with him, but it never came close to matching our lovemaking. It was never as good with him as it is with you."

He grins. "Good, that's good to know. You've salvaged my male ego. I couldn't stand the thought of you two being together. Other than me, he's the only other guy you've ever been serious about. When I called you and you were with him, or about to go be with him, it would drive me up the freaking wall. I had no claim to you, but that's how I felt."

"Well, certainly you weren't a saint out in L.A. All those models and..."

He puts a finger to my lips. "Shh. Squash that. None of those women could touch you. *None.* At the time I left, I thought it would be better for us to see other people. I preferred that it ended like that than for us to end up drifting apart and becoming strangers."

"But you see how we fell back together so quickly when you got back today. As soon as you stepped into the kitchen... Knowing the bond that we have, it was a mistake to get involved with other people. I was thinking about that today. For the past three months, I've been holding on to the lie that I was the wronged party in my relationship with Jaime. But it hit me that I was the one in the wrong since I wanted nothing more than to be with you again one day. That means that I pretty much used him as a fill-in until then. And I had the nerve to call myself retaliating against him for the shit he did."

"I wasn't fair to that girl Melanie, which is why I finally ended things with her. We could be out having a good time, and I would think, 'Dang, I wish Nik was here.' Now how unfair is that? I knew I had to end it when I was picturing you while I was in bed with her. We can't undo what we've done. We can only go about changing what we do in the future, which is build one together and not use other people as stand-ins. We're meant to be together."

"I want that more than anything, Mario."

"You know what you have to do then, right?"

"Move to L.A."

"Right. It's not only for us; it's for your career also."

"I recognize that. It's going to be so hard to leave. Rosie's the main reason I haven't left yet. A couple of years ago, I asked if she'd be willing to relocate. She wasn't down for it. I couldn't leave because Rosie needs me."

"Rosie needs you, or you need Rosie?"

I pause. "Both, I guess. When we were kids in NYC, we promised that we'd always be there for each other. After what her mother did to her, I promised that I'd never leave her."

"You were kids when you made those promises, Nik. You both have to live your lives as best for you; even if it's not with each other. Other than you, Chico's my best friend. Do you think it was easy to leave him? Or my parents, for that matter? It wasn't, but I had to do it. It's going to be hard for you, no doubt. But you have to do this, or you'll end up regretting it. You can't waste any more time, baby."

"I know," I whisper. "I know."

"Nik, you and I have always been straight up with each other, right?"

"Yes."

"Okay. Even though not wanting to leave your cousin is a big part of the reason that you've put off doing this, I think another part is fear."

"Fear?"

"Fear of what could happen or, rather, what could not happen. It's cool that you've been doing the play scene here and you've built up experience and a fan base. Coming to L.A. is a helluva risk. Everybody out there seems to be trying to break into acting. You've got mad talent, but there are others with just as much talent and they haven't been able to make it happen, for whatever reason. I'm not going to lie to you. There's that chance that you'll be one of those that can't catch that break. Your folks have always given you shit about your acting; saying that you're wasting your time. You're afraid that if you do this and fail, you'll feel your parents were right and that you've been wasting your time all these years."

I feel tears roll down my cheek. Mario sits up on one elbow and wipes the tears away with his hand.

"Baby, I'm not trying to hurt you by saying this. I merely want you to be honest with yourself. No matter what happens, anything that you do that brings you as much joy and satisfaction as acting does, is never a waste of time. I realize you want to be successful and famous and all that. You've got to go for it or you'll regret it forever. I love you and I believe in you as much as you believe in me. I hate seeing you put off what you need to do, year after year. You gotta roll that dice."

"You're right. Everything you've said is true. I don't like hearing my fears verbalized, but I'm glad you did it and I love you for it."

He pulls me into a tight embrace.

"This is going to sound corny as hell, but I want you to follow your dreams."

"And I will, Mario. I promise. Before my fears make me hesitate again."

We lie there quiet for a few minutes. Then I start giggling.

"What's so funny?"

"You. I suddenly remembered what you said when you first got here. Talking about how you have two bedrooms; knowing damn well we'll only be using one."

"That's true." He blushes. "Hey, you can't talk. You had the basement all fixed up for me to stay down there when you know I'm going to be right here every night."

"Guilty."

He stretches and yawns. "Any idea on when you'll make that move?"

"Within the next month."

"Promise me again."

"I promise."

"Like I said, I've got your back."

"No, you've only got my front. There's not enough lube in the world for me to let you put that horse dick back there."

He chortles. "As soon as I said that, I knew you were going to play on my words."

"Well…" I yawn. "I'd jump on you and ride you silly, but I'm beat right now. I guess you did a PTATS."

"What's that?"

"Put That Ass To Sleep."

"Oh." He grins at me. "We'll finish wearing each other out later."

We kiss one last time before drifting off to sleep in each other's arms.

CHAPTER NINE / *Nueve*

I awaken to the sound of someone crying loudly. I realize it's Rosie. Mario wakes up also. We stare at each other, puzzled. I jump up and grab my robe off the chair. My heart's racing. Mario throws on his pants. We hurriedly rush to the door. When I open it, Rosie's on the floor up against the wall opposite my room, holding the cordless phone. Crystal's standing in the doorway of Rosie's bedroom. She glances at Mario and me and shrugs her shoulders as if to say she doesn't know what's going on. I look at Rosie and tears are streaming down her face.

"No!" she cries. "*¡¡Dios querido, por que?!*"

"Rosie, what's wrong?" I ask.

"Do they know who did it and why?" she sobs.

My legs feel weak and my heart feels like it's going to break out of my chest. I grab onto Mario's hand. Tears start falling from my eyes. I don't even know why I'm crying, but something terrible has happened because Rosie rarely cries. I want her to put down the damn phone and tell me what's going on. At the same time, I want nothing more than to be back in bed with Mario waking me up, telling me that I was having a nightmare. Suddenly, Rosie throws the phone down the hall, startling the three of us. I release Mario's hand and sit down next to Rosie.

"Rosie." My voice is shaking. "What's wrong? Please tell us."

"There was a sh-sh-shooting," she sobs.

"A shooting?"

"Is it Chico?" Mario asks. I can see the panic in his eyes. Rosie doesn't say anything. She looks like she's going into shock.

"Rosie, was it Chico?" Mario asks again, his tone more urgent.

"No." She takes a deep breath. "It was Rhonda."

"Rhonda?" I whisper.

"She's gone, Nik. She's gone."

I'm stunned.

"Nooooooo!!!" Crystal wails. She slides down the doorframe to the floor, crying.

Mario comes and sits next to me, holding my shaking hand.

"What happened?" he asks, his voice cracking.

"That was Mr. Gibson. He and Mrs. Gibson are on their way to the hospital from the airport. They received the call earlier." Rosie's voice has suddenly become eerily calm. "Somebody shot up Rhonda and Dante's house."

"Why?!" I ask.

"Dante," she spits. "That motherfucker owed some guys some money. I guess they got tired of waiting. I knew nothing good would come out of her being with him. I knew it!"

Crystal gets up and sits next to Rosie. We all sit there, huddled together, letting what Rosie has said sink in.

"I can't believe this," Mario says in a hushed tone.

"Mr. Gibson said that Dante told him that Rhonda had a craving in the middle of the night and he got up with her. They were sitting in the dining room when it happened."

"So Dante didn't get hit? Oh my God. How's Jada?" I ask.

"Dante got shot in the leg and in the shoulder. Unfortunately, he's going to make it. As for Jada, they had to take her from Rhonda and they're trying to save her now. Mr. Gibson said that the doctors don't seem too optimistic. We've got to get to the hospital and see her. Come on." She stands up.

We all get dressed and get into Crystal's Mountaineer. Mario calls Chico's cell phone to tell him what happened and the name of the hospital. It goes to his voice mail so Mario leaves a message. For the rest of the ride, we're all silent. I glance at my watch and can't believe it's only 7:15. Almost twenty-four hours ago, I was waking up to prepare for the baby shower. Less than ten hours ago, I was hugging Rhonda and telling her I loved her. Now that I think about it, even though Rhonda and I were close and loved each other like sisters, I can count on one hand how many times we told each other that. It was one of those unspoken, yet known things between us. I'm so glad that that's the last thing I said to her.

A few hours ago, my biggest concern was breaking the news to Rosie that I was leaving for L.A. Now I'm dealing with the loss of my dearest friend. And, unless God has other plans, Jada as well.

CHAPTER TEN / *Diez*

When we arrive at the hospital, Rosie goes to the information desk and finds out where we are to go. They give us visitor badges to stick on. We take the elevator to the third floor. As soon as we step off, we see that Mr. and Mrs. Gibson have already arrived. Mrs. Gibson's sobbing on Mr. Gibson's shoulder. He's holding her with one arm and using the other to support himself with a cane. A doctor's standing next to them. He pats Mr. Gibson on his arm and walks away. We know the news without being told. We walk over to them. Mrs. Gibson spots us and lifts her head from Mr. Gibson's shoulder. It feels like someone has hit me in the stomach. I've always told Rhonda how much she and her mother look alike, but seeing her mother now, the similarity is almost more than I can take. I'm the closest to her and she lets go of Mr. Gibson and takes me in her arms.

"My little grandbaby didn't make it, Nicole," she cries. She and my late grandfather are the only ones who called me Nicole, instead of Nik or Nikki. "I've lost both of my babies. Both of my babies are gone," she wails.

I hold on to her tightly.

All of us take turns comforting her, as well as Mr. Gibson. While he's trying to be strong for Mrs. Gibson, he's on the verge of breaking down. Rhonda wasn't like a daughter to him—she was his daughter.

I'm still hoping I'm in the middle of a nightmare and that I'll wake at any time and trip on the terrible dream that I had. Then I'll go about my day as normal and I'll call Rhonda, talking some more about the baby shower, and she'll tell me to come over. I'll go over to her house and help her put together the nursery, with all the gifts, and we'll work on the thank you cards. Then we'll sit and watch a tape of the television judge shows that we both liked so much and pig out on pizza with everything on it. We'll engage in our usual gossip and I'll tell her the details of my night with Mario.

But that's not going to happen because for some reason God has seen fit to take not only Rhonda, but her child as well. I'm really trying to understand why a so-called merciful God could let this happen. Why didn't Dante die? It was because of him that this happened. No, instead He chose that Rhonda and her innocent baby should pay the price for the shit Dante had gotten caught up in. Why? Why God? Give me one of those famous signs of yours and let me know something.

9:50 a.m.

Mr. Gibson's about to take Mrs. Gibson home, where she can take a sedative. He's finally talked her into leaving. Chico arrived at the hospital a short time ago. He had his phone off and he finally turned it on and got the message from Mario. He seems to be in shock. I haven't seen him cry yet; he appears too stunned. Mrs. Gibson's decided that she wants to see her grandbaby before leaving. Mr. Gibson tries to talk her out of it, but she insists. Rosie, Chico, and Crystal go with her. I want to be there to support her, but I can't bring myself to go see Jada. I can't do it. Mario's sitting next to Mr. Gibson, with his arm around his shoulder. I ask them if they want some coffee. Mr. Gibson says that he does so I get up to go and find a vending machine.

I get on the elevator to go downstairs. There's probably a machine on this floor somewhere, but I need to get away for a minute. As I step off the elevator, I catch a glimpse of Junior, Dante's cousin. He and a woman are walking toward the waiting area where they speak to some other people. I walk to the hall that they walked away from. I go to the first room and look in—Dante's not there. I go into four more before I locate him. I walk over to him. His eyes are closed. His right leg is bandaged right above the knee and elevated on a pillow. A bandage on his shoulder is slightly showing through his hospital gown. Wake up, you bastard, so I can tell you exactly what I think of you. How you deserve to be the one dead.

You have no right to still be among the living. You fucking *hijo de pu...* His eyes open and he looks at me. Everything that I want to say to him is suddenly caught in my throat. His eyes are brimming with such anguish and pain.

"I know what you wanna say," he whispers. "It ain't nothing I ain't already said to myself." Tears begin to fall down the sides of his face. "It's my fault that the woman I loved more than life itself and my little girl are dead. I can't feel any lower than I do right now; I never will. But if it'll make you feel better to tell me what a worthless piece of shit I am, then go on ahead."

I stare at him for a minute. As fucked up as it all is, his gambling problem and what has happened as a result of it, I realize that he truly loved Rhonda and the baby. I guess my dislike of what Dante's addiction caused him to do blinded me to the positive side of their relationship. Take his gambling addiction out of the equation and you had a man who doted on and adored his woman. I can feel his pain. Damn it, I don't want to, but I can. I suddenly have the urge to reach out and comfort him. But I don't. Instead, I turn and leave the room.

As I walk down the hall, I remember Rhonda telling me that after they found out about the baby, he barely let her lift a finger around the house to cook or clean. Every night he would come home from work and either cook for her or bring her something to eat. I think back to yesterday at the baby shower. He took a break from playing Dominoes and came over and sat next to Rhonda. He put her feet in his lap, slipped off her sandals and lovingly massaged her feet. He didn't care who saw him do it; his boys or whoever. Rhonda was always talking about the sweet things he did for her and how no man treated her like he did. I hate to admit it, but I can now understand a little bit more why she stayed with him, despite his problem.

We arrive back at the house shortly before noon. I open the blinds in the living room and light fills the room. There's no sign of it raining again like it did last night. It's a bright and sunny day. After what's happened, it feels like a slap in the face for the sun to shine. Crystal goes upstairs; everyone else settles down on the couches. I take the tray from off the coffee table and go to the kitchen and clear it off. I get some glasses from the cabinet, fill them with orange juice, and go back to the living room. I set the tray on the table and sit down between Mario and Chico. Crystal's back downstairs and she and Rosie are sitting where they were last night. I get a flash of the scene I'd witnessed. I shake the image from my head. I ain't even trying to think about that right about now.

"I hope Mr. and Mrs. Gibson are going to be okay," Rosie says. "What we're feeling is nothing compared to what they must be going through."

"I know," I say. "Losing their only child and grandchild."

"I still can't believe this," Crystal says softly. "We were just feeling on Rhonda's belly and feeling the baby kicking."

"Yeah." Mario sighs.

"I want to go back to the hospital and see that motherfucker Dante," Rosie says.

"I saw him," I say.

"When?" Rosie asks.

"When I went to get Mr. Gibson some coffee. I saw Junior and went looking in the area that he walked from. I looked in the rooms till I finally found Dante."

"Mr. Gibson said that all his ass got was an exit wound in the leg and a grazed bullet in the shoulder. Can you believe that shit? You told his ass off, up and down and sideways, didn't you?"

"That was my intention."

"What do you mean, that was your 'intention?' Was his ass sedated or something and you couldn't say anything to him?"

"No, he was conscious. I didn't say anything to him."

"Why the fuck not?"

I say nothing. Rosie rolls her eyes up to the ceiling and takes a couple of deep breaths. She looks back at me.

"That *pendejo*," she says through clenched teeth, "is the reason that our best friend and her baby aren't here and you mean to fucking tell me that you said nothing?!"

"That's what I'm telling you. *Mira*, I was going to give it to him with both barrels, but damn it, I couldn't."

"Why the hell not?!"

"When I first walked in that room, I wanted nothing more than to send him to hell with the sheer power of my words, but he was already there. If you'd seen the look in his eyes, like I did." I pause before going on. "Then you would've seen that he really loved Rhonda and the baby. He has to spend the rest of his life with the fact that they're no longer here because of some shit he got mixed up in."

"That's the goddamn point. He still has the rest of his life. Rhonda and Jada don't. You're un-fucking-believable, Nik."

"Look, Rosie," Mario interjects. "It wouldn't have done any good to cuss out Dante. It's not going to bring them back."

"I'm talking to my cousin, Mario. You stay out of it."

"Don't tell him to stay out of it! He's right. Me cussing that nigga out isn't going to bring them back."

"You picked the wrong time and person to play the role of Ms. Sympathy, Nik. That motherfucker doesn't deserve one bit of understanding! Why you gotta be so goddamn soft?!"

"Why do you always have to be so motherfucking hardcore and shit?! Sometimes you gotta put yourself in someone else's shoes and see what they're going through; even if it's the last thing you want to do!"

"Hell fucking no! I ain't trying to play devil's advocate for someone whose actions caused my friend to die!"

"Both of y'all shut the hell up!" shouts Chico.

We all look at him. I still haven't seen him cry yet, but now he looks like he's finally about to. His lower lip is quivering. I put my hand on his leg. Right then a tear rolls down his cheek. Rosie and I look at each other and silently agree to call a truce. We all fall silent again. No one has yet to touch the orange juice.

"Well," I say, standing up. "I'm going to take a shower and get started on those calls for Mr. and Mrs. Gibson—letting people know."

"I called Odell from the hospital," Rosie says. "I think he was in shock; he barely said two words. But he should be over soon."

"Nikki," Crystal says. "I can help if you want."

"Yeah, thanks, Crys."

"Have you seen my pager anywhere? I looked upstairs for it and didn't see it."

"No." I don't know why she's worried about a damn pager right now.

Crystal starts checking between the cushions and Rosie helps her. I grudgingly go look around the dining room and then the kitchen. A few minutes later she and Rosie come into the kitchen.

"Any luck?" Crystal asks.

"Nope."

"Shoot! I hope I didn't drop it outside anywhere. It'll be ruined since it rained last night."

"Let's go look," Rosie says.

She and Crystal head toward the steps leading down to the back door. I follow behind them. We step outside and stop in our tracks. We look at the decorations from the baby shower that we didn't get a chance to clear away last night. Some of the balloons have burst but others haven't and they're swaying in the light breeze. A cardboard stand-up stork has fallen back against the garage. Pink and yellow streamers are wet on the fence and bushes. The tables, covered with colored paper tablecloths, are drenched with moisture. I turn and go back into the house and get some garbage bags. I come back out and the three of us begin to clear all remnants of the baby shower away in silence.

CHAPTER ELEVEN / *Once*

"Something smells good as hell," Rosie says as she enters the kitchen.

"Thanks," I say. "I haven't made paella in a while because it takes so much time to prepare. I decided to cook it 'cause I needed something to distract me for a while. There were still so many leftovers that Mrs. Gibson let us have from after the funeral, but I took them over to Ms. Delia. You know she's raising damn near all her grandkids and she was really thankful. I hope you don't mind that I did that."

"No," she says, sucking her teeth. "You know I'm like you on that. I don't care for food from after a funeral. The first day is fine, but after that it's almost like an extra reminder, you know?"

"Yeah."

Rosie goes and sits on a chair at the kitchen island. "Nik, you never did see Jada," she says softly.

"I'm glad they did a closed casket for her. I wouldn't have been able to handle it, Rosie." I turn around from the stove and look at her. "What did she look like?"

"You know how most babies look like freaking aliens? Well, all prejudice aside, she was beautiful. She looked exactly like those baby pictures of Rhonda."

I feel a swell in my chest. I don't want to cry anymore. The last time I cried so much was when my grandparents died. Rosie was the stoic one. She cried once and then after that, she consoled me. The last few days, we've been taking turns consoling each other. The funeral was a double one and seeing Jada's little casket next to Rhonda's was too much for everyone. Mario broke down crying. I'd never seen him cry like that. It had broken my heart even more.

"You know," I say as I go sit next to her, "I'm still surprised at what you did with Dante."

"Nik, if you don't quit talking about that shit, I swear to God, I'm going to pop you. I don't want to talk about it."

"But…"

"Ah! What did I say? It was simply a temporary lapse of good sense."

"Mmm-hmm. Whatever."

Even though there had been a lot of anger directed at Dante for the shooting, seeing him at the funeral melted even the most cold, vengeful heart. He was on crutches and he went to Rhonda's casket and kissed her on the forehead and repeatedly said how sorry he was. When he got to Jada's casket, he laid his hand on it and was so overcome, his friend Omar had to help hold him up. When I saw him going down the aisle when we were leaving the church, he looked like the walking dead. I think that if someone had walked up to him and stabbed him in the chest, he wouldn't have even felt it.

It was at the cemetery that I finally did what I felt like doing at the hospital but didn't—I hugged him. I felt that if Rhonda's parents could find it in their hearts to reach out and comfort him, then I could also. Plus, I knew that Rhonda would've wanted me to do that. Rosie had been standing next to me and I just knew that when I turned back around from hugging Dante, she was going to be shooting daggers from her eyes to me. Instead she surprised the shit out of me, God, and everyone else when she walked up to Dante and hugged him, too. Dante was surprised as well. When she first went toward him, he looked like he was bracing himself to be hit. For the most part, my cousin's a hard ass, but she's also got a lot of heart.

"I'm still tripping on those cousins of Rhonda's," I say.

"Hell yeah. That little skinny bird-faced one leading the pack gonna go up to Mrs. Gibson and say that the family should be in the first row instead of us."

"She looked so cheap when Mrs. Gibson said, 'The family is in the front row.'"

"Rhonda's biological father seemed pretty hit."

"Didn't he? He looked pitiful. He seemed lost in his own world—didn't say much to anybody."

"Probably eaten up with guilt over not being a bigger part of Rhonda's life and such an asshole in the little part that he was."

"Yep. Anyway, let's change the subject. I don't want to talk anymore about the funeral."

"Okay, me either."

We sit there silent for a few moments.

"So," I finally say, grinning at her.

"Soooo what? What are you grinning at me like a Cheshire cat for?"

"So what was it like throwing down with Alejandro and Crystal?"

"I figured your ass wasn't out the entire time."

"Well, what was it like getting it on with the two people you care for?"

"Wait a minute. Were you awake to see when Crystal was doing her thing with me?"

"Yeah."

"And you weren't surprised by that?"

"Not really."

"What? I don't know why not 'cause shit, I was. I couldn't believe it when she kissed me and then felt up my *tetas*. I almost passed out from shock when she started munching on my carpet."

I chuckle. "Rhonda told me something earlier that day. I promised not to tell anyone since she didn't want the information leak to be traced back to her. But it doesn't really matter at this point. She told me that Crystal had gotten caught in bed with Omar's brother Jalil's wife."

Rosie's jaw drops open, then she smiles and shakes her head.

"Are you sure, Nik?"

"Yeah, why?"

"'Cause, after Alejandro left and me and her finished doing our thing, she fucking told me that she couldn't believe what had happened, that she'd never done anything like that before, and how it must've been the liquor and the weed."

"Uh-uh. No she didn't."

"Yes. I didn't really buy it 'cause girlfriend knew her way around the punani a little too well to have been brand-new to the game."

"That's Crystal; forever playing the innocent. You didn't answer my question. How was it being with the two people you care about at the same time?"

"You know." She sighs. "I was the one who suggested that we do it and I was geeked when they both agreed. I was like dang; it's going to be the bomb. And it was—sort of."

"Sort of?"

"Yeah, when I was grooving with both of them, that shit was beautiful. But when them two started going at it and left me on the sidelines, it brought the whole thing down. Sitting there watching them screwing sucked. And you know what was worse than seeing them fucking?"

"What?"

"Seeing them kissing. And hearing Alejandro calling her baby like he did. I felt shut out and jealous like you wouldn't believe. We had a good time after he left though."

"Why did he leave?"

"You know that workaholic. He had to work the next morning."

"After Rhonda told me about Crystal, I was worried that you and she would do something, you'd fall in love even more, and end up hurt."

"Rosaura ain't gonna end up hurt. Trust that."

"That's good to know, Odell."

"Why you call me that?"

"You sounding like him, referring to yourself in the third person."

"Oh." She chuckles. "Anyway, you worry too much."

"Yeah, I do sometimes. I'm guilty."

"Hold up, it suddenly hit me what you said about me falling in love even more. The word love never came from my lips as far as Crystal's concerned. I said I had some feelings for the bitch and I wanted to fuck her."

"I could've sworn that you said you loved her."

She holds her hand up. "Boop, boop! Uh, no. That's you saying all that love shit. I merely had a high-level crush."

"You sure you didn't say you were in love with her."

"Nikki, I'm sure that I didn't. You know how your ass exaggerates shit sometimes. Dramatic!"

"Oh, brother. I don't know where I got that from then."

"Me either."

"I figured that's why you were dragging your feet with Alejandro; 'cause you were carrying this torch for Crystal."

She puts a hand on her hip. "Where the fuck did you get that idea? If I'm dragging my feet with Alejandro, it's because I ain't never been serious about anybody. I'm extra cautious and he was rushing things." She pushes my shoulder. "Silly."

"Oops!" I giggle.

"I don't regret what happened. It opened my eyes to some things."

"Like?"

"Even though I need some time, I think I'll give Alejandro a chance."

"I'm happy to hear that. What made you finally decide to give him a shot?"

"It hit me when I saw how jealous I was, when he was getting it on with Crystal. As for Crystal, I'm really turned off by her pretending like she hadn't done that before. She was trying to make me feel guilty and almost made it seem like I'd plied her with drugs and alcohol and had taken advantage of her. Hell, everything she did, she did on her own. If you down for some shit, simply admit it. I hate fakeness like that."

"Come on now, Rosie. Why you acting brand-new? You know Crystal's always been a bit fake with hers."

"You're right."

"You and Alejandro will be so good together."

"I think we will, if he can be cool with me being with a woman from time to time."

"I'm sure he wouldn't mind, if you let him in on the deal."

"Oh no. I told you how I felt the other night. That ménage a trois shit is for people who are emotionally uninvolved. That's my personal opinion. Enough of getting all up in my business. Mario's been camped out in your room instead of downstairs."

I blush. "Mmm-hmm."

"Look at you, sitting there eating cheese. Is it still good, Mami? Is it still good?"

"Yes! Girl, if anything, it's even better than before. We haven't done anything since that first night, because, well you know. But it was just...just...explosive!"

"Ole Mario laying that pipe on my cousin. Aw suki suki now."

"Rosie, that nigga knows how to work it. Shit, and I needed it, too. I was sick of buying batteries all the time. Hector's cool, but it can't replace the feel of the flesh of a man."

Rosie giggles. Then we're quiet for a few moments.

"What are you thinking about?" she asks.

"I feel kind of funny; that's all. I suddenly realized that when all of us were here getting our freak on around the same time Rhonda was..."

"There's no use in thinking about that and feeling guilty, okay? We're trying to get our minds off that for a bit, so let's not go there."

"You're right."

"Sex has surely been the last thing on your mind; mine too, but since Mario's leaving next week, you'd better stock up on that *pinga* before he goes." She nudges my shoulder with hers.

"If I'm still not in the mood by the time he leaves, it's no problem 'cause I'll be getting it on the regular when I get out to Cali." *Fuck! I could just smack myself in the mouth!*

"Oh, you're planning on going out there for a vacation or something? 'Cause if you are, let me know when and I'll take some time off and go with you. I'd like to visit there."

I don't know if I should put off telling Rosie and merely play it off for now, like I'm simply going out there for a vacation, or tell her of my plans right here and now.

"Yoo hoo!" Rosie waves her hand back and forth in front of my face.

I still don't say anything.

"Nikki, what's wrong with you? Oh, I get it. You two will probably want to be alone for a change and I might be in the way, right? It's cool. I'll get a hotel room. I can get a good discounted rate with this service I signed up with through my credit card and that way..."

"Rosie, I'm not going out there for a vacation. I'm moving out there."

Rosie looks like I slapped her.

"You're what?"

"I'm moving there."

"Moving there for what?"

"I need to actively pursue my acting career."

"You are pursuing your career. Look at all the plays and local commercials you've done."

"Exactly, Rosie. The key word is 'local.' And even though I've loved doing that, I want to do more. I want to do films—directing and producing them as well as acting in them. And that ain't gonna happen here."

"Nikki, there are a lot of actors from here who've made it. Jeff Daniels, Tim Allen, that chick Selma Blair..."

"Yeah, there are a lot of actors from here that have made it. But they didn't make it here. They had to go elsewhere, like New York or California. That's what I've got to do."

"You can't do this to me, Nikki!" Rosie slams her fist down on the island counter-top. "You can't leave me now! Damn it! I buried one of my best friends two days ago. I couldn't take you leaving on top of that!"

Tears start streaming down her face. I feel the tears coming to my eyes as well.

"Nikki," she says, her voice soft now. "We've always been together. Always—from the cradle. We got our nasty diapers changed together, our snotty noses wiped together, we had our first Communion together." She grabs my hand. "We even had our first kiss together, when we cornered Tony Muniz in the coat closet and made him kiss us. Remember?"

"Yes." I grin as I wipe away a tear with my other hand.

"Even before we lived in the same house, we were never more than five minutes from each other. Now you're talking about moving thousands of miles away from me. I've never known what it was like for you not to be with me—and I don't want to know."

"Then why don't you come out to L.A. with me? Mario has a spare room. He won't mind. I trust Chico to look after the house."

She's quiet for a moment.

"The thing is, Nik, this guy Vito and I are making moves to open a gentleman's club together. He already owns a couple in Atlanta and he's ready to bring one here. It's going to be a partnership where he puts up the capital and I'll be responsible for selecting the dancers and pretty much running the place. If we get this off the ground, it'll be a hell of an opportunity. Plus, I want to see how it's gonna play out with Alejandro..." Rosie pauses and smiles weakly. "I suddenly realized something."

"What's that?"

"I sound like a real selfish bitch right now. I'm going on and on about the shit I want to do and... You've gotta do what you've gotta do. We both have to. I only wish we could do it together, *mi 'ja.*"

"Me, too." I slide off the stool and pull her up to hug her.

"I'm gonna miss your crazy ass so much, Nikki."

"I'm gonna miss you, too."

She hugs me tighter. *"Te amo mi prima, mi hermana."*

I feel even more tears fall down my face. *"Te amo."*

We stand there hugging a bit longer before finally breaking apart. I reach over and get a napkin from the counter and I give her one as well.

"Listen, it's not like we'll never see each. You can come out any time you want. And it won't be easy, but I'll come back here as much as I can."

"So when are you planning on moving?"

"Within the next month."

"Why so soon?!"

"Rosie, I've been putting this off for the longest. I need to hurry up and do it before I find another reason to procrastinate. After we found out about Rhonda, I was going to put it off again, but Mario said that I should stick to my original timeline. If I don't do it now, I'll never do it. And I'm not getting any younger, you know?"

"I understand. How are you getting out there? Driving?"

"Shit no. I'm not doing all that driving. I'm catching a plane. I'm having everything shipped out there. My clothes, books, and other personal stuff won't be that much. It's shipping my car and bike out there that's going to make my bank account cry the blues."

"Well, I've got some paper saved. If you need some help, let me know."

"Thanks, Rosie. I'm not trying to wish any bad luck on you or anything, but if things don't work out here like you plan, will you consider moving to L.A. then?"

"Hmm. I've never really had much interest before in living out there, but if shit don't pop off like I want it to, I'd be game to give a shot."

"I might see your ugly ass out there real soon, if *Playboy* chooses you to pose for them. I can see it now. You out there, chilling with Hef at the mansion, and you and him fighting over the bunnies."

"Shut up, heifer."

I turn and check the paella.

"Ever since we heard about Rhonda, I've been going to bed crying myself to sleep in Mario's arms. Tonight, I want it to be different. I want for us to try and get back some semblance of normalcy. When my grandparents died, Mami said that it's best to try and get back to a normal routine as soon as possible because if you don't, you'll wallow in sadness. And you're not doing your loved ones any good by doing that. Rhonda and Jada will always live in our hearts."

"That's true. I think this past week I've made up for all the crying that I didn't do in my life."

"Well, tonight we're going to eat some of what I'm sure is delicious paella and kick back and relax. Mario and Chico are visiting their relatives and will be back soon. I'm going to go to the store and get some yak for Mario." I turn the eye on the stove down a little lower. "Keep an eye on this for me, okay?"

"Sure."

"Do you want anything from the store?"

"Yeah, get me a pack of Salem Lights."

"All right." I start out of the kitchen, then I turn and give Rosie a kiss on the cheek.

"Get your mushy ass on out of here." She grins, though her eyes look sad.

CHAPTER TWELVE / *Doce*

After I leave the store, I notice I'm almost on empty so I stop at the BP gas station. Black Peoples Gas, as we call it. I get out my credit card and pump the gas. I finish and get back in the car. Right when I put the key in the ignition, I realize I forgot Rosie's cigarettes when I went to the store. I get out and go inside to get them. As I walk back to my car, I have my head down putting the cigarettes in my purse. I hear a familiar voice behind me.

"Long time, no see."

I turn around and look right into Jaime's face. He's shaved off all of his facial hair. A lot of times when a man looks good with facial hair and he shaves it off, he doesn't look as good. But Jaime's face is still handsome—it simply has more of a boyish appeal to it.

"Hi, Jaime. How have you been?"

"Good, good. Believe it or not, I was on my way to see you."

"Really?"

"Yeah. I just left Fairlane. I had to get Moms a birthday gift and I was gonna stop by and see how you were doing. I recently returned from our family reunion in New Orleans and I heard about your girl Rhonda. I'm sorry to hear about what happened. She was good people. I really hated to hear that the baby didn't make it."

"Thank you, Jaime. I appreciate that."

"I know y'all was tight and it's gotta be hard."

I nod my head.

"Give Rosie and Chico my condolences also."

"I will."

He looks down for a moment. "But, um, other than that with your friend, everything going okay for you?"

"Yes. I'm about to move out to L.A. within the next few weeks."

"For real? Straight up?"

"Yes. I'm going to get on the ball and go after my acting full throttle."

"Man, so you 'bout to book up out the D. Much luck, much success."

"Thanks."

"L.A., huh? You'll be right out there with your boy Mario. You gonna be living anywhere near him?"

"Well," I say hesitantly. "Actually I'm going to be living with him. He's here now visiting."

"Oh." There's a flicker of hurt in his eyes. "He's staying at your place, I take it."

"Yeah."

"I guess it's a good thing we ran into each other like this and I didn't just drop by your crib like I planned. I ain't even tryin' to run into that dude."

"Why?"

"Why? Nikki, I ain't got no desire to run up on a nigga that I've always felt I was competing with. The entire time we were together, it was Mario this and Mario that."

"I never threw him in your face, Jaime. I don't even remember mentioning him all that often in front of you."

"Yeah, but when you did, your face would light up. What man wants to see his woman react like that at the mention of some other nigga's name? Even though his ass was all the way on the left coast, he might as well have been right here— between us. I always felt like I was sloppy seconds next to him and the first chance you got to be with him, you would. Now tell me that things between y'all are strictly platonic and y'all ain't picked up where y'all left off."

I say nothing, just look down to the ground.

"That's what I thought," he says. "Nik, I ain't trying to make excuses for the dirt that I did, but I could never really commit to you like I wanted to since I knew you weren't truly committed to me. And that shit hurt like hell."

I look up at him. "I'm so sorry, Jaime. I am. I did love you. A part of me still does and always will love you."

"Just not like you love him."

I don't say anything.

"It's cool. It ain't like I didn't already know. You females ain't got the lock on intuition. I was wrong for messing around on you and I'm man enough to finally admit it and apologize for it."

"Thank you. To paraphrase Chris Rock, 'I ain't saying what you did was right, but I understand.'"

We both smile.

"Outta curiosity, how did you find out that I had somebody over that night? Y'all came with bats ready and everything."

"That cheap ass 99 cents store phone of yours with the tricky redial," I say, smiling. "When Antoine was calling another number, he accidentally called me."

"Aw!" He covers his face with his hands. "I was wondering... See, I busted myself 'cause if I hadn't called back to tell you about the tickets *and* to make sure you were nice and tucked into bed, Antoine would've redialed his own number, since his was the one I dialed before you."

"Mmm-hmm," I say, shaking my finger at him. "By the way, I want to apologize for the yard work."

"Oh, man, you got me back good. I wanted to strangle you and your cousin so bad. But I almost ended up killing those boys next door to me—Roshaun and Kamari. That morning they were on they porch laughing their asses off. They said they heard the commotion when you and Rosie were knocking on the door trying to get in, and they figured y'all did that to my yard. I'm standing on my porch, pissed as hell, and them niggas were over there rolling. I guess it was kind of payback for them 'cause I was always getting on them about stepping on my grass and shit. It was kinda funny when I think about it now but, at the time, I was mad as hell."

We both smile, then fall silent.

"Again, I'm sorry, Jaime." I reach out and stroke his bare cheek. "I'm sorry for everything."

"This is gonna sound cliche like a mutha, but we had some good times, right?"

"We had some great times; we really did."

We stare into each other's eyes, giving each other looks of apology mixed with regret.

"I feel like we're having a B-movie moment." He grins. "Can I get me a hug, girl?" He opens his arms.

I go to him and we embrace. As I hold him, I become enveloped in his warmth and familiar scent. I don't get flashes of that night when I got back from PR, but the good times that we had. Snuggled up watching horror movies, driving to Ohio to go to Cedar Point amusement park, riding our bikes together. And the time when we had planned a Saturday picnic and it decided to rain. He said for me to get the basket ready 'cause we were going to have our picnic anyway. He picked me up and brought me to his house, and in front of his fireplace, he had the blanket spread out and ready. He had candles on the floor and some wine chilling in a bucket. He'd even gone to Gags 'N Gifts and got some plastic ants. He said that you couldn't have a picnic without them.

My memories and our embrace are interrupted when some guys in a passing car heckle us.

"Go get a room at the Ramada, nigga!"

"I ain't mad atcha, dawg! Ow!!"

I shake my head and look back at Jaime. "I'm going to go before I cry for the millionth time this week. You take care, Jaime."

"You too, girl. I'll be looking for you at the show. I don't doubt that you'll make it. You've got skills."

"Thanks. That means a lot." I kiss him lightly on the lips, then walk back to my car.

As I pull off, he's still standing there watching me. I raise my hand and wave and he does the same. I'm so glad that things are right between Jaime and me. We won't be ace boons, but at least there's no animosity still lingering. I'd made up my mind that I was going to go over to see Jaime before I left town anyway. Rosie would call me a straight-up flower child for saying this, but I'm about to enter a new phase in my life. I didn't want there to be any unresolved issues from my past that could bring bad karma to my future. Overall, Jaime's a great guy and he deserves a woman who'll love him and only him—fully and completely. It's funny when I think about it—the beginning of Jaime's and my relationship was hearing his voice from behind in a store and the closure of it was the same way, in the parking lot of Black Peoples Gas. Funny.

CHAPTER THIRTEEN / *Trece*

Sunday, August 12, 2001, 11:25 a.m.

It's a lazy Sunday morning and I'm still lying in bed. It's been two weeks since Mario left to go back to L.A. I missed him before he even left. We did end up making love again the night before he was to leave. Our lovemaking was both animalistic and romantic. One minute we were going at it buck wild doggy-style, and the next we'd tenderly look into each other's eyes as he thrust into me sweetly and gently.

As if to have extra assurance that I wasn't going to back down on my promise to relocate, a couple of days before he left, Mario brought home some boxes and boxing tape. We started packing up some of my things. Rosie came home a short time later and stuck her head in my bedroom door to say hello. She saw what we were doing and a slightly stricken look crossed her face. The conflict of emotions overcame me again. I'd been feeling excited and happy about my move to L.A. but seeing the look on Rosie's face made me feel a great sadness of leaving here. Mario must've known what I was thinking. He came and sat next to me on the floor and put his arm around me. He didn't say anything for a minute; he silently comforted me.

"Nik, did I tell you that you're going to be fifteen minutes from the beach?"

I blushed at him. "Are you trying to entice me even more with waves and sand?"

"Yep. You've always wanted to learn how to surf. Now you can."

"That's something else to look forward to. I can't wait to tackle those waves. I'll probably be out there so much, I'll get nice and dark like Mami."

"I've been out there a few times. My neighbor Ben and his wife, Lisa, are surfing fanatics and they gave me some lessons."

"Man, that's cool."

He leaned over and gave me a kiss.

"You don't know how happy I am that you're finally moving out there."

"I'm happy, too. I'm still sad to be leaving Rosie and Chico and everybody, but I feel really good about this."

He picked up a roll of package tape, took my left wrist and put it next to his right one, and taped them together.

I looked at him and raised my eyebrows up and down. "Kinky."

He grinned. "This was supposed to be symbolic."

"I was only playing. But, Mario, you may want to remove this tape real gentle like because you've got this sticky tape right on the hair on your wrist."

"Oh, fuck!"

I shake my head and smile at the memory. The sound of the phone ringing snaps me out of my reverie. I glance at the caller ID. It says *Moreno, Miguel L.* Oh great. It's one of my parents. I was going to have to tell them of my plans sooner or later. I might as well get the shit over with. I pick up the phone.

"Hello."

"Zuzu."

"Hi, Papi."

"What are you doing?"

"Nothing."

"I was calling to see how you were. Your mother and I haven't heard from you in over a week. Are you doing all right?"

Well, if you really must know, my heart's racing faster than a car on the Autobahn and my mouth's dry as hell. You're going to fucking trip over what I'm about to tell you.

"Yes, Papi. I'm fine. How are you and Mami doing?"

"We're doing good, but you'd know how we were doing, had you bothered to call."

I roll my eyes.

"Your mother and I just got back from Mass. Something I'm sure you and Rosie haven't been to in a while."

"Papi, please don't nag me about that."

"If you did like you were supposed to, I wouldn't have to nag. Have you spoken to your *abuela?*"

"Yes, I called and spoke to her on Friday."

"You called your *abuela* in Puerto Rico but you can't pick up the phone to call your parents in New York?"

"Papi..."

"Never mind. It's because she spoils you and doesn't give lectures like I do. Listen, your mother and I were talking about what to do for our vacation around Labor Day. We're thinking of coming there to visit. You don't have other plans, do you?"

Boy, do I.

"Well, actually Papi...Umm."

"What, Zuzu? What's going on with you? You've sounded strange ever since you answered the phone."

"There's something that I need to tell you."

"What? You're not pregnant, are you?"

"No!"

"Well, what is it? Hurry up. You know this is long distance."

"Oh please, Papi. You've got a phone plan where you only pay two cents a minute. I could keep you on the phone till Tuesday and you'd only owe five dollars."

"Will you quit being a smart aleck and tell me what's going on."

"I'm moving out to L.A. to further pursue my acting career." The words rush out of my mouth so fast that it sounds like one big multi-syllabic word. I don't hear anything for a few seconds. I close my eyes and brace myself for the verbal maelstrom.

"Nikki, what the hell are you talking about?"

Uh-oh, he called me Nikki instead of Zuzu. He only calls me Nikki when he's upset with me.

"You heard me, Papi. Next Friday's my last day at Quinn Investigations. I'm moving to California a week later."

"When the hell were you going to tell your mother and me?!"

"I've been putting it off because I knew what your reaction would be."

"How in the hell are we supposed to react, Nikki? Are we supposed to be happy that you're leaving your job, your friends and family, and not to mention the beautiful home that your grandparents left to you, all so you can go chase some silly pipe dream? How can I have a daughter who's so intelligent, yet so stupid at the same time?!"

Tears sting my eyes and I feel that awful sensation in my chest and stomach that comes when someone hurts your feelings.

"This is why your mother and I have never approved of you doing this acting stuff. You've always been a bit rebellious and we were afraid that you'd do something crazy like this. You hear all the time how people go out to Hollywood, trying to be movie stars and end up waiting tables, or worse, they end up doing porno movies and getting into prostitution and drugs. And we're supposed to be happy with this? Where are you going to live and how are you planning to support yourself until you win your Oscar?"

Oh, joy. Now he's opened up the can of sarcasm.

"I've sent my resume to a temporary agency out there to get me set up until I can find something steady; until I can make some leeway with my acting. And I'll be staying with Mario."

"Super. Not only are you going out there to try to be an actress, but you're going to be shacking up as well. Living in sin in the city of sin."

Papi's words really hurt at first. But now that hurt has been replaced with a steely resolve and defiance.

"Look, Father." He's not the only to switch up names when he's angry. I call him "Father" instead of Papi when I'm mad at him. "First of all, the city of sin is Las Vegas. And what difference does it make that I'm going to be shacking up? In case you're under some grand delusion, let me tell you right now that I haven't been a virgin for close to ten years."

"Nikki!"

"Don't Nikki me. Now you listen. I'm not going out to L.A. to try and be an actress. I am an actress; now I want to become a known and successful one. What you said about what happens to some people who go out there to act is true. But it isn't always true. Damn near every actor in the business who became successful started out waiting tables and if that's what I end up doing, then so be it. I realize you don't agree with what I'm doing, but that's too bad. I'd love to have your blessing on this, but if I don't, it's not going to stop me. I cannot and I will not live my life for you and Mami. The bottom line is I'm going after something that makes me happy. And I would *not* be happy living my life the way you want me to!"

"I think you're making a big mistake. When your mother was your age, she'd settled down, gotten married, and had you. And you would've had brothers and sisters, if God had been willing."

"And?"

"Don't you think it's time for you to settle down, too? You should find yourself a nice young man there in Detroit to marry and start on a family, instead of running off after a foolish dream."

"Okay, your argument suddenly lost all credibility. That's some straight-up fifties sh... *Mi Dios!* You do realize we're in the millennium, don't you? You can be old-fashioned at times, but this is ridiculous. If it were up to you, I'd be twirling around the house in high heels and pearls and marveling over the shine of my kitchen floors and getting dinner ready for Wally and the Beave. Mami never let you get away with that junk with her so don't try to use me to spout off your retro ideas and values."

"Young lady, you can be flippant all you want, but the fact is you need structure in your life. Maybe if you and your cousin would start back going to Mass and get more involved in your religion, you two wouldn't be so wild."

"You ever stop to think that our religion is what made us wild? All of the restrictions and the no-nos. Don't drink, don't smoke; what do you do?" Like my father would know the lyrics to "Goody Two Shoes" by Adam Ant.

"You stop that blasphemous talk right now!"

"Okay, I'm sorry. Look, the fact is I refuse to wake up one day, fifty years old and regretting that I didn't at least take a shot at this. I'm going to try to make you understand something that it seems you and Mami have never been able to. And that is why I love acting so much. It's my calling and it's my passion. It's such a great feeling to slip into the shoes of a character; especially one that's nothing like me, and give that character life. Such life that the audience believes I am who I'm portraying."

I pause for a moment before going on.

"I remember one time, I did this play when I was eighteen, and my character was this villain. After the play, I and some other members of the cast were hanging out by the stage door and these girls walked by and shouted, 'Laura is a bitch!' And they meant it, too. At first I was taken aback, but then I realized that I'd taken some dialogue from paper and made it into someone who people had such a strong reaction to; even it was negative. I can't describe how good it feels when I'm able to make people laugh, cry, love, or hate the person I'm playing. I'm talented at what I do. That's not being egomaniacal; it's being truthful. This is a gift that God has given me and I'm ready to take it as far as I can. Up till this point, I've taken it only so far because I was afraid to leave my comfort zone and risk not attaining the success that I want. I have to do this, Papi—I'm going to do this. If you can't accept it, then at least please try to understand."

Papi doesn't say anything for a few moments.

"I don't agree with what you're doing. I don't agree at all, but it looks like you're determined to do it. You've always been stubborn, when you set your mind to something. I guess that's something you inherited from me. I can't give you my blessing, but I'll pray that things work out the way you want them to."

I'm having a Terry McMillan moment. It feels like I've been holding my breath the entire conversation and, finally, I exhale.

"I'll take that, Papi. That's better than nothing."

"I've seen you act and you're very gifted. I've never denied that you are. I simply don't see much of a future in it. Like I said, I'll pray that it goes okay."

"Thanks."

"It's not going to sit well with your mother; especially you leaving that house."

"I know."

"I'll try to tell her the best way I can. I guess she's finished making lunch and I'm starving. So I'll talk to you later. You be good; or at least try to be. Tell Rosie I said hello."

"I will."

"Be sure to let us know your new number and address."

"Of course. I'm sure you want to eat so I'll call back and give it to you. I love you, Papi."

"Yeah, yeah." He clears his throat. "Me, too. Uh, bye."

"Bye-bye."

I obviously get my mushiness from Mami. Papi loves me; he's simply not verbally demonstrative of that fact. He's always been more comfortable showing me that he loves me by doing things, or buying stuff for me, than actually spitting those three words.

Dang, I'm glad that's over with. It wasn't as painful as I thought it would be. I glance at the clock. It's barely past noon, so it's about 9:00 a.m. Mario's time. He gets up pretty early sometimes. I think I'll give him a call and hope that I don't wake him. I dial his number.

"Hello?"

"Good morning."

"Nikki?"

"The one and only."

"Damn, I was just thinking about you."

"Uh-huh."

"I was. I'm stroking a major boner right now."

"Okay, now I believe you." I smile. "I called to give you some great news. I finally told my father of my plans."

"What? That's good, baby. You feel a lot better, don't you?"

"Yes. It was rocky at first. He kind of tore up my little feelings a bit. But I came back with it and he actually kinda, sorta accepted it—a little. Hey, that doesn't sound like much, but I was happy to get that."

"I'm happy for you. Two more weeks and my baby will be out here with me."

"I can't wait, baby. I miss you."

"I miss you, too."

"Mmm. You sound even sexier in the morning. You've got that extra huskiness to your voice."

"Thank you."

"You were really stroking yourself, huh?"

"Mmm-hmm. I still am. I was thinking about when I had that ass all up in the air and was hitting from the back, banging it. What do you have on, baby?"

"A T-shirt."

"That's all?"

"Yeah. You know I don't sleep in panties."

"Shit. Yeah, I remember. Touch yourself for me, Nik."

"I already am," I purr.

Mario turns me on so much that I felt myself getting wet when I first heard the sound of his voice. My legs are open and I'm stroking my clit in small circles with my middle finger.

"Do you love this punani?"

"Hell yeah, I love it."

"Tell me what you love about it."

"It's so nice and tight. I love the way it grips my dick and how it gets so damn wet."

"It's really wet right now, baby."

"I can't wait to taste it again; bury my face in it. Flick my tongue against that hard little clit. You miss this dick, don't you?"

"Yes, you know I do," I whisper.

"If you were here right now, how would you want me to be fucking you?"

"Oooo, baby. I'd want you to be slamming this punani with that big ass dick. Beating it up, giving it to me fast and hard."

"Yeah, you'd have those long ass legs wrapped around my waist or up on my shoulders. Mmm."

"I want you so bad, Mario."

"Mmm, Nik. I wish you were licking and sucking on my balls right now. Shit, I love it when you do that."

I hear the creaking sound of my door opening. Fuck! I forgot to lock it.

"Time to get up, gi..." Rosie says as she suddenly stops from entering the room any further.

I drop the phone as I rush to cover myself with the sheet.

"Dang it, Rosie!"

She turns to face the hallway. "Uh, sorry. I was coming to tell you that I'm almost finished cooking and that Odell's downstairs. You come on down when you get finished. Tell Mario I said hello." She closes the door, cracking up.

I pick up the phone. "Hello."

"Well, that made me as soft as cotton candy at the State Fair," Mario says, laughing.

"You heard me getting busted?"

"Yep. Better you than me."

"Thanks." I finally find the humor and begin snickering. "At least it wasn't Chico."

"Really. I wouldn't want my brother seeing my woman playing with herself."

"Your woman?"

"Yeah. You're my woman, aren't you?"

"We've never made it official. I sure wouldn't mind being asked." I start humming. "Nope, sure wouldn't mind at all."

"All right." He chuckles. "Nikki, will you officially be my woman?"

"Yes, honey, I will."

"Good. Can I start telling you that I love you?"

"Yes," I say softly.

"I love you."

"I love you, too."

"I have a small calendar where I'm marking off the days till you're here."

"You do?"

"Um-hmm. Okay, baby, I better get started on this article. I gotta do some research for it."

"All right. I'm going to hop in the shower. We'll talk later."

"Yeah, let's finish talking tonight. Be sure to lock your door this time." He chuckles. "I love you."

"You best believe the door will be locked. I love you, too. Later."

CHAPTER FOURTEEN / *Catorce*

After I shower and put on some clothes, I head downstairs. As I walk through the living room, I hear voices coming from the kitchen. When I enter the dining room, Odell sees me, walks and stands in the doorway of the kitchen. He throws his right hip to the side, puts a hand on it, and looks me up and down.

"I hope you na washed yo' hands and ain't comin' up in this kitchen with cooty cat sauce on yo' fingas."

Rosie bends over the stove, giggling. I stop in my tracks, put my hands on my hips, and glare at Odell. I break out laughing and continue walking to the kitchen. I walk up to Odell and give him a hug.

"Hey, crazy."

"Hey, yo'self. I told Miss Rosie to go on upstairs and let you know I was here. She said you was up there in bed with the phone in one hand and the ill na na in the other."

"Rosie, you ain't have to tell my business."

"Hell, you've caught me doing a whole lot more than sticking my hand in the cookie jar."

"You and Mario havin' phone sex?" Odell asks.

"Yes."

"I like that Mario," Odell says. "Y'all make a good couple. I thought you and Jaime were okay together, but you and Mario gotta little extra somethin' somethin'."

"You know what I think of most men," Rosie comments. "They ain't 'bout shit. Mario's an exception. And I hope Alejandro is, too."

"Ohhh!" Odell says as he fans himself with his hand. "I love me some Alejandra! Now Nikki, yo' man is fine, but Alejandra is fiinnneee!" he sing-songs. "He's my other dream man; other than Michael Jackson."

"Okay," I say, holding up my hand. "I've never, ever, ever, ever understood this thing you have for Michael Jackson. I don't get it. He's like the most a-sexual person, next to the Pope."

"Really," Rosie adds. "Alejandro—yeah. I totally understand that 'cause that nigga's fine as hell. But Michael Jackson? How you do go from Alejandro to Jacko?"

"I don't care what you two hens say. I been in love with Michael since I was a chile."

"If you had the chance, you'd actually have sex with him?" I ask.

"I sho in the shit would. Girl, I'd suck the bleach offa his dick."

"Uh-uh!" Rosie and I say together, laughing.

"I would," he says, reaching for the bag of chips on the counter.

"What-ev-er," Rosie says. "Nikki, I forgot to tell you that Crystal and I got into it last night."

"Over what?" I ask.

"She wants to do it again with Alejandro."

"I thought her ass was supposedly so drunk and high that she didn't mean for all that to happen."

"She meant when me and her got down. She must've had all her senses when she was fucking Alejandro. Last night we were talking and she said that Alejandro was really good..."

"Uh, uh, uh, I bet he was, chile," Odell remarks coyly.

Rosie says, "Will you let me finish, Senorita Hot Cock? She said that Alejandro was really good and wanted to know if I'd mind if the two of them got together for another session—without me."

I was stunned. "She didn't!"

"Oh..." Odell puts his hand to his mouth. "Miss Crystal know she wrong for that."

"Her ass had the nerve to say that since me and Alejandro weren't serious, I shouldn't mind. If I was turned off by her ass before..."

I interrupt. "What did you tell her?"

"I told her hell to the no! I said that Alejandro and I are moving toward a relationship and any more menageries were out of the question. Then she acts like she's gonna cop an attitude and comes at me with, 'It's a waste of time for him to be with you because you're gay. He needs a woman like me.'"

"No!" I exclaim.

"That trick done lost her mind," Odell says, looking at me.

"I said, 'For your information, I'm bisexual. Aren't you?' She said, 'I'm not bisexual, I'm straight. I love dick.' I said, 'You may love dick but you like pussy also.' She said, 'That was a one-time thing.'"

"Ooh!" I say. "Her lying ass."

"I said, 'Crystal, you mean to tell me that I'm the first and only woman you've been with?' She said, 'Yeah! I've never done anything like that before, and I wouldn't have if you hadn't come on to me when I was high.' I had to hold my tongue so hard I almost bit it off. Even though Rhonda's gone, I still didn't want to tell her what I knew. So I said, 'I was down to sex you, but I wasn't going to do anything unless I got the green light. And I did 'cause you initiated the physical shit between us. You were eating me out like a pro. I'd put down money that you'd done it before. I can tell when it's a bitch's first lick.' She got all flustered. 'I don't know what you're talking about. I don't even remember all that.' I said, 'Funny how you've got amnesia on the shit we did, but you remember every inch of Alejandro's dick.'"

Odell and I chuckle.

"She said, 'Just forget the whole thing.' I told her that won't be any problem. Fuck that *sucia.*"

"We know that she's been with Jalil's wife," I say, "and Yvette and who knows who else. I don't know why she didn't want to get with both of y'all again. Unless it's because she likes Alejandro in more than a sexual way."

Rosie has a quizzical look on her face. "What do you mean, she's been with Yvette? Which Yvette?"

"Your Yvette—the chick from the hair salon. I didn't tell you about that?"

"No, you didn't. Fill me in."

"The day of the baby shower, Crystal was here in the kitchen trying to get the scoop on Alejandro and other things. She said that when Yvette did her hair, she told her all about you and her."

"No fucking way!"

"Yep."

"Ain't no way that girl would've spilled that to Crystal, unless they were fucking or she knew Crystal was down for that also."

"That's what I figured. Yvette was paranoid about anyone finding out about you two."

"Crystal and Yvette. Small world, ain't it?" Odell nods his head and snacks on some potato chips.

"Shut up, fool." Rosie grabs a chip out his hand and tosses it at him. "Anyway, I don't know why Crystal ain't trying to get a two-for-one deal with me and Alejandro. Not that she could get another one. She *clearly* loved getting down with me. She needs to quit trying to blame it on being high. Hell, she took a shower and that should've cleared her head a little. After that, she came back in the room for some more. It wasn't until her ass was tired from fucking that she started in on that, 'What have I done?' bullshit. Who knows about her? She's one of those people you can know your whole life and don't know them at all. I ain't putting any more energy into trying to figure her ass out. I can't believe I had some feelings for her."

I shake my head. "I don't know what to say about her."

"Like they say…" Odell states. "Denial ain't just a river in Egypt."

"Ain't that the truth," Rosie says. "Odell, when are you moving in with Jamal?"

"Next weekend, chile. I can't wait. Roberta's getting on my last nerve. I can barely stand to look at him. I was feelin' a little guilty about leavin' him, but I sho ain't now."

"What has he been doing?" I ask.

"Nothin' really. When you ain't feelin' somebody anymo', everything they do is irritating. I hate the way he eats, the way he slurps when he drinks somethin', the way he always scratchin' his nuts…"

"Oh no!" I chuckle and glance over at the stove. "Odell, even though it's summer, there's about to be a blizzard. I couldn't believe it when Rosie interrupted me from doing my business to tell me that you were here and that she cooked."

"I know, girl," he says. "And ain't nobody had to beg or drag her by the titties to the kitchen. She cooked on her own. You feelin' all right, Miss Rosie?"

Odell and I look at her, smiling.

"Fuck both of y'all. I don't mind cooking every once in a while. I just ain't trying to be all Martha Stewart with the shit every day."

I walk over and inspect the pots.

"Mmm. Chicken and dumplings, green beans—and not beans from a can either—and corn. And you made some rolls. Chico will be happy. He loves chicken and dumplings."

"That's really who I made it for. I'm hoping that it'll cheer him up some. Rhonda's death hit us all pretty hard, but it seems like it hit him even harder. He's been in his room most of the time since the funeral."

I agree. "I tried to talk to him and tell that we have to go on; we can't wallow in grief. He was like this when he and Mario's grandmother passed away. Mario called and asked me to go over to his apartment and check on him 'cause hardly anyone could reach him by phone. He completely shut down and it took him a while to get back to normal. He's still in his room?"

"Not upstairs. He started moving stuff downstairs last night and this morning. He's going to be staying down there from now on."

"Oh yeah, he mentioned that he was going to do that. Well, I'm going to go and try talking to him again. I hate to see him like this."

I head down the steps to the basement. Chico has put up a Japanese Shoji screen for more privacy.

"Hey, Chico. Can I come in?"

"Sure, Nik."

I step around the screen and he's sitting in the recliner, reading a book. Jean-Luc Ponty is playing low on the stereo. He's burning one of the coconut-scented incense sticks I gave him. I sit down on the end of the sofa bed closest to him.

"How are you doing, Chico?"

"Fine."

His eyes don't leave the book.

"Reading another Walter Mosley book, huh?"

"Yep."

This isn't going to be easy.

"Rosie's making one of your favorite dishes: chicken and dumplings."

"I knew I smelled something good."

"I like the way you've got it set up down here."

"I'm not finished yet. I still want to do a couple other things."

"Where did you get those prints?"

He has two on the wall, opposite the sofa bed. One is of a black man and woman, nude and embracing, and the other is a Native American woman, also nude and covering strategic areas with her hands.

"I got them at this gallery downtown."

"They're really tasteful."

"Thanks."

I sit there for a minute or two before saying anything else.

"Are you going to miss me?"

His eyes finally leave the book and fall upon me. "Of course I will, Nikki. I'm gonna miss you like crazy. Why would you even ask me that?"

"Well, you know that I'm leaving in a couple of weeks and you haven't been spending any time with me before I leave."

He places the book down on the table next to the recliner.

"I'm sorry, Nik. I've been lost in my own world. I ain't never been good at handling losing people close to me; whether it's from death or from them moving away. In the last few years, I've lost Nana, Mario, Rhonda and the baby, and now you." He grins and looks down. "I probably sound like a little bitch."

"No, no, Chico. Not at all." I reach out and take his hand in mine.

"Nikki, I've got something that's been eating me up inside. If I don't get it out and tell somebody I feel like I'ma explode."

"What is it, sweetheart?"

He lets go of my hand, stands up, and gets something out of the bottom of his entertainment center. He comes back and sits down. He has a Bible. He holds it out in the palm of his right hand.

"Put your hand on it, Nikki."

I look at him and then the Bible. I place my hand on it.

"I'm 'bout to tell you something that I ain't told another soul; not even my brother. You've got to swear not to repeat what I'm about to tell you."

"All right. I swear I won't tell anyone."

He takes the Bible and places it on the table. What he has to tell me must be a doozy. Most of the time, if Chico wants to tell you something that he doesn't want you to repeat, he'll only accept a verbal promise. But if it's something deep, he'll pull out the King James.

"Nikki, there's a strong possibility that Jada could've been my daughter."

I open my mouth to say something. What, I don't know. It may be a good thing that I don't quite know what to say, since my vocal cords don't seem like they'd cooperate anyway. Chico stares at me as I struggle to find the words and then speak them.

"Remember when Rhonda broke up with Dante, after he'd staged that break-in?"

I nod my head. My mouth's still hanging open.

"You know she made him take her to the pawn shops where he'd taken a lot of the stuff, right?"

I nod again.

"One of the things was this television/stereo system with speakers and a receiver that he'd bought for them. The night after he left, she called and asked if I could come over and hook it back up for her 'cause she didn't know what wire went where. I went over there the next day after work and did it. She was really down about that entire situation. She was crying, saying that she loved Dante, and she'd tried so hard to be patient with his gambling problem. I tried to comfort her as much as I could. I went out and brought back some Chinese food. After we ate, she went and got out some Jack Daniel's and Coke. We flung back so many drinks that we killed the bottle. I was trying to help her into bed, and ended up in bed with her."

He sighs and runs his hand across his head. He must've not shaved it in a few days. He has a lot of stubble. Why am I thinking about his stubble? Am I in some kind of mild shock?

"Anyway, as wasted as I was, I managed to get it up more than once that night. We both woke up feeling awkward like you can't imagine. She was in love with Dante, and I loved Rhonda, but I wasn't in love with her. Of course she ended up taking Dante back a couple days later. Not too long after that she found out she was pregnant."

I feel like I can finally say something. "It could've still been Dante's baby."

"Yeah, it could've been, but I doubt it. Don't you think it's strange that they were together all that time, yet the minute she and I sleep together she gets pregnant?"

"Yeah, that's true."

"Also, I saw that baby, remember? Even though she looked a lot like Rhonda, she looked a bit like me also. I didn't see anything about her that looked like Dante. Rosie made this comment about her, too. She said, 'Look, Chico, she's got ears just like you.' I'm sure she didn't think twice of it, but it almost made my knees buckle. I wish to God that I'd stayed in the waiting room with you, Mario and Mr. Gibson. I can't get Jada out of my head. I wouldn't have been able to anyway, but it's made it harder to have actually seen her."

I take a breath. "Did you talk to Rhonda about that possibly being your baby?"

"Yeah, but she didn't want to hear that. She'd made her mind up that she was having Dante's baby. She was in total denial that it could be mine. Since she felt so strongly about it, I decided to go along with what she wanted."

Suddenly, I get a memory flash of the baby shower. "That's what that look was all about!"

"What look? What're you talking 'bout?"

"At the baby shower, when we were all feeling Rhonda's stomach. When you felt it, you and she exchanged the strangest look. I didn't think anything about it, but now it's clicking, and it makes perfect sense."

"Yeah, that was a weird moment. I wasn't even going to feel her stomach at first, but everyone else was doing it and it would've called attention if I didn't."

"I'm so sorry, Chico. What you must've been going through. It hurt us all, what happened to Rhonda, but knowing that you've been dealing with the possibility of having lost a daughter as well as a friend..."

"No, Nik. Bump that possibility and coulda been junk. I don't even know why I said that. 'Cause I know." He pats his chest. "That was my daughter. I feel it in my bones. I know. I know."

His eyes well up with tears. I get up and sit in his lap. I wrap one arm around his shoulders and, with my other hand, I hold his face to my chest. He hugs me tightly. Though my heart is breaking for my friend, I cried so much when Rhonda and the baby died that my tears are dried up for now. I simply rock him and comfort him.

After a few minutes he loosens his grip on me. "Nik, can you get up a minute?"

"Sure." I get up and sit back on the sofa bed.

"You're heavier than you look." He stretches and rubs the leg I've been sitting on.

"Oh, bite me." I reach over and wipe the tears from his face with my hands. Then I take his head in my hands and plant a quick kiss on his lips. "I love you, man."

"I love you, too," he says sheepishly.

"One thing that Rhonda's death has taught me is to let the ones I love know that I love them more often."

"I hear that. On another note, I'm glad they have one of the two guys involved in the shooting in custody."

"Yeah, me too. That's somewhat of a relief. Too bad Michigan doesn't have the death penalty."

"For real. If anybody should get hit with some high voltage, it's those mofos. I saw Omar at the gym yesterday. He said Dante was staying with him, but now he's down in Alabama. He might end up staying down there. He couldn't go back to the house afterward, except to get his stuff."

"I don't blame him. I wouldn't be able to go back there after that either. Did Omar say how he's doing?"

"He wasn't good at all. That nigga had a fucked-up problem but he loved the shit outta Rhonda. No doubt."

"Knowing that has made it a bit easier not to hold a grudge against him."

"Hey, you two!" Rosie shouts down the stairs. "Come on and eat before greedy ass Odell eats up everything. She's acting like she's got a damn tapeworm or something."

"Shut up, crow!" I hear Odell say.

"Okay, we're coming!" I say.

Chico and I stand up. I give him a hug.

"Thanks for listening, Nik. That made me feel a lot better."

"You're more than welcome. I can run my mouth, but right now I'm at a loss for words."

"Like I said, listening helped. You don't have to say anything."

"Do you think you'll tell your brother?"

"Eventually."

"Well, you don't have to worry about me saying anything."

"I realize that." He pats his belly. "I am hungry. I haven't had anything to eat since yesterday afternoon."

We walk to the stairs and up to the kitchen. After what Chico has told me, I've got a lot more to digest than chicken and dumplings.

CHAPTER FIFTEEN / *Quince*

Friday, August 24, 2001, 2:50 p.m.

Today is the day. Last night Chico and Rosie gave me a going-away dinner at Flood's, a restaurant/bar/music joint. Odell, Alejandro and some friends from work, as well as some of my acting buddies were there. Crystal wasn't able to make it because her job took her out of town, but we had dinner together a couple of nights before she left. It was kind of awkward. She felt weird, knowing that I'd witnessed her having sex with Rosie and Alejandro. Rosie said Crystal was hoping that I'd been sleeping the entire time. Rosie let her know that I hadn't been. I wasn't too comfortable with Crystal either. She'd tried to make it seem like Rosie had taken advantage of her while she was drunk and high. I didn't appreciate that. They're barely on speaking terms now. I knew becoming intimate would compromise their friendship, but I thought that it would be because Rosie would get hurt. I'm glad that didn't happen, but I'm sorry that their relationship is in such shambles.

The day before my bike and car were shipped to California, Chico and I rode our bikes to Rhonda's and Jada's graves. He wanted me to go with him to put out fresh flowers. Chico and I spoke to her, both alone and together. Neither of us cried this time. In fact, we ended up tripping, talking about some of the crazy things we'd done; especially when we were teenagers. Like the time we all went driving out in the suburbs one summer night. We came across a lake and Rosie talked us into skinny dipping. We were having a great time, until we were awash in the floodlight from a cop car. We had to beg and plead with the officers, who threatened to take us all in for public indecency and trespassing on private property. Lucky for us, they gave us a break. Going to the grave also gave me an opportunity to tell my friend goodbye again. I told her to wish me luck and I promised her that I'd be back to visit her and Jada.

When we got back from the dinner last night, Rosie and I did something that we haven't done since we were kids. We slept in the same bed. I'd turned in and had barely gotten off the phone with Mario when she tapped on the door and asked if it was okay to come in. I told her that it was. She walked over and got under my covers. We talked about everything from Rhonda to Alejandro to Raul, who's going to be coming to visit in a couple of weeks. I hate that I'm going to miss seeing him. We lay talking, arm in arm, until about 5 o'clock this morning.

I'm sitting on my bed trying to gather the strength to get through one of the hardest days of my life. I stand up and get my purse and my luggage by my bedroom door. I only have two suitcases since everything else has already been sent to L.A. I look around my room one last time. I pick up everything and head downstairs. I place my suitcases and purse down by the front door. I've arranged for a cab to pick me up; it should be here any minute. Rosie and Chico argued with me vehemently about it but I stood my ground. I don't want anyone to go to the airport with me. This was already going to be hard enough. I feel this way will be somewhat easier. Somewhat. Rosie, Odell, and Chico are sitting in the living room.

"You shoulda let me bring those down, Nikki," Chico says.

"It's okay. They're not that heavy."

Rosie's sitting next to Odell, with her elbows on her knees, staring down at the carpet.

"Come on, guys," I say, my voice slightly cracking. "I'm going to L.A.; not the gas chamber."

No one speaks a word.

"Sorry. That was a weak attempt at humor."

Odell gets up and comes over to me. "Don't you forget this diva when you become famous, Nikki Morena."

"Odell, please. Who do you think is going to be flying out on location to do my hair?"

Odell grins and his eyes begin to mist with tears. "That's right, you call on me.

Don't let none of them white hair stylists who don't know nothin' 'bout yo' kind of hair mess it up." He grabs me and we hug each other. "I love you, Miss Nikki."

"I love you, too, Odell."

"I ain't gonna say no mo' 'cause I'ma be tore up if I do."

Right then I hear a horn outside. Chico gets up and peeks out the window. "It's your ride," he says somberly. He goes over to my suitcases and takes them outside to the cab.

I reluctantly let Odell go. He turns and goes outside.

"Rosie?"

She slowly gets up and walks to me. She doesn't look at me; simply falls into my arms. She doesn't make any sound, but her body's shaking like she's sobbing. I feel a torrent of tears fall down my face. She lifts her head and gazes at me, her face wet with tears.

"What am I going to do without you, Nik?"

"Quit acting like this is the last time that we'll see each other. Didn't you say that you were going to try and fly out the weekend after Raul leaves?"

She nods and brushes a stray hair from my face.

"Even though I hate like hell that you're leaving, I realize you have to. I love you more than anybody on this earth, Nikki. You ain't never let me down. Never. You've always loved and accepted me, no matter what. I want you to know that I'd give my life for you. I swear to God I would. If you ever need me for anything, you pick up that goddamn phone and I'll be on the first plane out. You hear me?" I nod my head. "And if anybody tries to fuck with you in any way..." She chokes up.

"The phone works both ways. If you need me..." I can't go on either. I grab and hug her again. "Rosie, I gotta get out of here, before I completely lose it, okay?"

I let her go and turn to walk to the door. She grabs my hand and we look at each other for a moment.

"Your mushy ass gonna step up outta here without telling me you love me?" she asks, smiling through her tears.

I squeeze her hand. "I love you, Rosie."

"I love you, Nik."

I let go of her hand, turn, and walk to the door. Odell's standing on the porch with his arms folded and Chico's by the cab.

"Take care of yourself, Odell." I give him a peck on the lips. Tears are streaking his face.

"I will, girl. You, too." He reaches out and strokes my arm, then turns his head, facing the house next door.

I walk down the steps to the cab.

"Chico," I say, grabbing him.

We hug each other tightly and he lifts me off the ground for a moment.

"My bro is gonna take good care of you. Last few times I talked to him, all he was going on about was you coming there."

"I'm going to take good care of him also; don't you worry." I kiss him on both cheeks and on the lips. "Call me whenever, okay? Anytime you want to talk—about Jada or whatever."

"I will. I love you, man."

"I love you, too, man."

"I put your purse in the back seat."

"Thank you."

I let him go and he opens the door for me. I look back and see Rosie and Odell standing on the porch. They have their arms around each other. I grin and wave. They do the same. I get in the cab and Chico closes the door and steps back on the grass. We wave at each other. The cab driver pulls off.

Leaving everyone I know and love here has got to be the most painful, difficult thing that I've ever done. But all I can do now is look to what's ahead. I don't know exactly how this new chapter in my life is going to read, but I'm finally ready to find out.

ABOUT THE AUTHOR

Shelley Halima is a writer/lyricist/poet who was born in Charlotte, North Carolina and raised in Detroit, Michigan. Her passion for books and music began in childhood. In 2001, she resolved to realize her dream of becoming a writer. Since then she has completed a novel, short stories and over 100 poems and lyrics. *Azucar Moreno* is her first novel. Shelley currently resides in Metro Detroit and is working on her second book. She can be reached at shelleyhalima@yahoo.com.

EXCERPT FROM

Los Morenos

BY SHELLEY HALIMA

COMING SOON

Just as I start setting the table I hear Mario's key in the door. I walk around the corner to greet him. He looks dead tired, poor thing. After all these years of knowing him, it still bowls me over how gorgeous he is and how I attracted I am to him. He just cut his midnight-black curly hair a month ago, but already it looks like it's grown back. I've lost count of how many times my hands have caressed that field of curls. Or how many times I've gotten lost in his beautiful green eyes—mesmerized by the golden flecks dancing within them. Mmm, don't get me started on those sexy, slightly full lips. I can't imagine even after forty years that I'd tire of kissing them. I think the reason I haven't grown tired of his masculine beauty is that his spirit and intellect are even more beautiful. A man with a keen mind and a generous heart is automatically appealing and will do nothing but boost what he's got going on outside.

And if I may walk down Crass Street for a minute, him having a nice thick nine-incher that he knows how to work, sho don't hurt any, okay? Also, I love the casual/cool way he dresses. He has on beige Dockers, white shirt rolled up at the sleeves and brown suede loafers. His black messenger bag with his laptop in it is slung over his shoulder.

"Hey you."

He just turns the corners of his mouth down in a playful pout and opens his arms. I go to him and wrap my arms around him and feel his envelop me.

"What a day." He sighs.

"A rough one, huh?"

"Yeah, baby. I'm glad to be home."

I give him a peck on the lips. "Well, put down your bag, kick off your shoes and come eat some dinner and tell me all about it."

"Sounds good to me. I can taste on your lips that you've started on the after-dinner drink early."

"Ah, no lectures."

"It wasn't a lecture, just an observation. What are we having?"

"Porterhouse steaks, stuffed potatoes, salad and rolls."

"Mmm-hmm. That sounds good 'cause I'm starving."

He washes his hands in the kitchen sink while I put the food on the table. We both then sit down to eat. Mario says a quick blessing and proceeds to tear into his plate. I consider myself a thoroughly modern woman who will have my own career and not depend on a man for my livelihood. And I'm a woman who will only walk beside my man—not behind him. I have views that would make Glorias Steinem and Allred proud, but at the risk of putting my feminist card in jeopardy, I love taking care of my man and one of the ways I do that is by making him a delicious meal. It's reciprocal so it's all good. He pampers me, too. Breakfast is the meal that's his forte, and let me tell you his scrambled eggs put mine to shame.

"So, babe, tell me about what's going on at work."

"You know how we've got a new owner, right?"

"Yeah."

"At first we were all just happy that we were able to keep our jobs. But now it's been a battle with this dude to not turn the magazine into some big gossip and bling-bling rag. One of the reasons that I was happy to get a job at *Urban Report* is because of the quality of the articles, you know? They covered things that affect our communities like government policies and police brutality. It had entertainment articles but that was just a small part of what the magazine was about. Lloyd is trying to flip it and make it all about who's fucking who in show business and doing photo layouts of some celebrity's crib. He's steering away from what this magazine is all about. I'm not saying there shouldn't be a gossip column or interviews with singers, athletes and actors; we can have that, too, but our people need information that's going to empower us—especially the shit that doesn't get coverage on the evening news."

"I hear you, baby. I noticed a change in the previous issue but when I read the latest one that you left me to read this morning it had a lot more lightweight type of articles. And they pushed your article on Bush's latest policies way in the back of the damn magazine. I had to go through thirty stories about rappers and big-name jewelers and stuff like that to get to yours. I had to look on the cover a couple of times to make sure I was reading the right magazine."

"That's what I'm talking about. That shit infuriates the fuck outta me. They had a big ass story about where to buy diamonds instead of how we got peeps dying in Africa so that we can floss ice. Now I know why he turned down my article on the Sierra Leone. Before Diane retired, she would've had us writing about how stupid that kind of shit is, not glorifying it. I'm starting to feel like a hypocrite working at *Urban Report*. The stuff we were writing about were things to educate and try and guide our people away from this nonsense of chasing trinkets and baubles and to show that our focus should be on purchasing things like stock and land—something we can leave to our kids. What the fuck are we gonna leave to the next generation—rusted rims and diamond bracelets?"

I nod, smiling in agreement and admiration at the passion Mario has.

"What?" he asks, smiling back at me. "Am I going off on one of my tangents again?"

"Yes, but I love it. Your tangent is more than justified. I wholeheartedly agree."

"See that's what I'm saying." He makes an eye-to-eye gesture between us with his hand. "We right there. There might be some hope though. I heard from a couple of people who work fielding e-mails from our readers that many are complaining already about the content of the last issue and it just hit the stands. We're having a meeting next Tuesday and me and some of the other writers are going to try again to talk some sense into Lloyd and use those e-mails from readers to back us up. If that don't work and things keep going like they are, I'll start putting out my feelers for a new job. Once I'm sure where I stand on my j-o-b, we can start looking for a house. I know that we could get one now 'cause you got a steady gig, but I want to be able to contribute, too. We've outgrown this apartment and we need more space."

"Speaking of space, we're going to have someone taking up more space for a few weeks."

"Who?"

"Rosie. *Silk & Velvet* wants her to come out here for some test shots. I'm excited for her."

"Hmm."

"'Hmm'? What does that mean?"

"Nik, you know I love Rosie like a sister but I don't understand why she wants to be in one of those magazines. I know *Silk & Velvet* is one of the more classy skin mags, but it's still exploitive to women, don't you think?"

"It's what Rosie wants and I support her."

"You didn't answer my question—don't you think those magazines are exploitive to women?"

"I told you that my agent wanted me to pose for that very magazine."

"Thank God you didn't."

"Only because I couldn't work up the nerve and I knew you would've tripped."

"Damn straight. I bet you wouldn't like it if I posed for *Playgirl*. Nikki, you still didn't answer my question."

"Look, I'm not saying that I one hundred percent approve of posing for those magazines, but I'm not about to sit up in judgment of my cousin. Whatever makes her happy makes me happy."

"So even if she's exploiting her body, you're happy?"

The temperature of my blood has risen by a good ten degrees. He's starting to piss me off as well as dropping a notch or two off my buzz.

"Don't look at me like that, Nikki. I'm just asking a question. I know that Rosie went through a lot as a kid and you're protective of her…"

"Anyway," I say, cutting him off. "I'm going to New York on Saturday."

"To visit your parents?"

"That too. But mainly it's to meet Rosie there—her mother has cancer and she's going to see her finally. She wants me there with her. We should be back Sunday afternoon or early evening. She said she'll probably just come on out here with me."

"That's too bad about her mother."

"Yes it is."

"I hope she makes it through."

"Me too."

We finish the rest of the meal in silence. Even if he hadn't ticked me off, I wouldn't really want to talk about what's going on with my parents. Not right now anyway. I just want to do anything I can to not think about that. I get up and start clearing the dishes. As I'm rinsing off a plate before putting it in the dishwasher, Mario comes up behind, turns off the water and takes the plate from my hand and lays it in the sink. He puts his hands my hips and turns me around to face him.

"Look at me, baby."

I lift my head up at him.

"I didn't mean anything by what I said. I love Rosie and I'm not trying to put her down. I just think she's capable of doing more than showing off her body. I know she's back to dancing but before the feds went after that guy Vito and shut down all of his clubs, Rosie was almost single-handedly running the one in Michigan, right?"

"Yes, she was," I say as I reach over and dry my hands on a towel.

"That shows that she has a good business mind. Chico told me that she had the place packed damn near every night. She respects what you say and you should use your influence to guide her in a more productive direction. It was lucky for her that all the FBI did was question her and let her go. They could've tried to pin on her some of what they got Vito and some of his other partners on. It's not just you either. Tell me if I'm wrong, but it seemed like your folks gave you more grief about acting than they did her about dancing. While they were busy nagging you, they just ignored what Rosie was doing. Right?"

I don't say anything. What can I say? Mario is right.

"I've known the both of you since we were all kids. Your father was always the main one getting on you two for coming in late or getting into fights and whatever, but from what I could see you got punished more when it was just you doing something. I know for a fact that even though you were the quieter one and you followed Rosie into devilment, you pulled Rosie into a lot of stunts, too. And I think you did that 'cause you knew that if you got caught, the punishment wouldn't be as bad if she was involved. Tell me I'm wrong." He tilts his head, grinning at me.

"Whatever."

"Don't try to hold back that smile."

I finally give in to the smile tickling my lips. "Shut up. I hate how well you know me."

"I understand the fact you all were accommodating of Rosie because of her mother not being around. But instead of always co-signing on whatever she does, try and steer her to something else that's positive."

"You're forgetting how upset Papi was when he found that she was bisexual. Mami was dealt with it okay, but Papi didn't take it too well. He wanted me to move back home from the apartment Rosie and I were sharing."

"True. But that lasted a hot minute. After that he just turned a blind eye to it and tried to pretend that her bisexuality didn't exist."

"My family is pretty good at turning a blind eye to things we find uncomfortable to deal with. I think it's a genetic trait. I hear what you're saying. But I'm still going to support her if she does get chosen for this magazine. I refuse to put her down for it. It's not like someone is making her do this; she's doing it on her own."

"Is a hooker any less of a hooker if she doesn't have a pimp?"

"Hey, I know you're not calling my cousin..."

"No, I'm not calling her a hooker. I would never do that. I'm just saying it's not much a difference from exploiting yourself to someone making you exploit yourself. Okay, I'll keep my comments to myself as far as her posing nude and stuff. By the way, you know that I'm not trying to put her down, right? I'm only looking out."

"Yeah, I know. You made a good point."

"So, you're not mad at me, are you?"

"No, idiot."

"Good, 'cause I really need some tonight."

I giggle and punch him lightly in the stomach. "You're so nasty."

As he leans in to kiss me, he whispers, "You know you like it."

"I never said I didn't. Just making an observation..."

EXCERPT FROM

Love's Game

BY HAROLD L. TURLEY II
PUBLISHED BY STREBOR BOOKS INTERNATIONAL

LEARNED FROM THE BEST

E very little boy has one cousin or uncle in their family they look up to and
want to emulate. Mine was my older cousin Terry. I wanted to dress like him,
play basketball as good as him, but most of all I wanted to have all the girls
that he had.

I remember, when I was younger, he had his girl Tracy over to the house. I was staying
over for the weekend because he was taking me to Triples Nightclub on Saturday to
see the Junkyard Band. I saw him rush out the door, go downstairs, and then come
back upstairs with a disturbed look on his face. He came into the back room with me
while I was playing Nintendo.

"Go in my room and ask Tracy to show you how to work the computer," he said.

"But why? You already showed me earlier today."

"I know that but she doesn't. Just do what I said and stop askin' so many damn
questions. Oh, play dumb too, so she can break it down for you. I need about a
good fifteen minutes."

I didn't understand what was going on but I agreed.

"All right!" I replied.

He then went downstairs and I went into the room and asked Tracy what he had
told me to ask her. Sure enough, she was more than willing to show me. About
twenty minutes had passed, and in walked Terry with a slight sweat.

"Damn, boo! A nigga's missin' you. Can't I get some luvin?"

She looked at him with a smile filled with joy and was more than happy to oblige him. They both darted into the bedroom and closed the door. I knew what time it was, so Terry was going to be in there for at least two hours. Puzzled by why Terry was acting so strangely, I went over to the window and looked outside. I saw Ebony getting into her car. Ebony was the chick Terry had met about two or three weeks prior at the Safari Club.

It turns out that Terry had gotten his times mixed up with Tracy. He had forgotten that she was coming over early that day, so he had told Ebony to swing by. Terry had it that way; he never had unexpected visitors. He made sure all of his girls called him before coming over. How he did it? Hell if I knew. Later I found out that Ebony had called and said that she was up the street and on her way. Terry had me keep Tracy company while he went downstairs and had sex with Ebony in the basement. He knew that Tracy wouldn't have any problems showing me how to use the computer and that would give him the time he needed.

After he finished with Ebony he didn't just rush her out the house. No, he cuddled a little bit with her and told her that he had to pick his mother up from work so he had to get ready to go. He used the bathroom downstairs to wash off so Tracy wouldn't smell Ebony's scent on him. He told Ebony to go ahead and let herself out, like he was in a rush or running late so she wouldn't press him, came upstairs, and took Tracy right into the room so she wouldn't happen to look out the window and see Ebony getting in her car. He fucked both of them that day. The nigga was smooth, I mean *smooth!*

Terry was always introducing me to all the right people. He had just been drafted by the Boston Celtics when I was in junior high school. It didn't just stop with basketball; he was much smarter than that. He made sure he knew any and everybody. He knew NFL players, club owners, and entertainers. I probably knew more people by the age of fourteen than most people would ever meet. Shit, I even knew damn doctors and lawyers. Terry knew anybody that was somebody in D.C. and, after a while, so did I.

He taught me the two most important things in life; how to manage my money and my women. I had a couple of candy scams working at school from my locker and a different girl to call my own. They all went to different schools throughout the D.C area.

"Never mess with a girl that goes to school with you because everybody will know your business," he would tell me.

When a girl has a boyfriend that goes to another school and someone wants to know about them, usually she will tell them, *"You don't know him. He goes to another school."* Then the subject is dropped and your name is never brought up. See, this is important because you never know who knows who when it comes to girls. Everybody knows somebody! The chances of getting caught were slim to none, if you ask me.

Shit like that is what he taught me throughout my childhood; the ends and outs of how to be a playa. I only wish he'd taught me the ends and outs of how to be a man instead but like all things, you have to learn the hard way...

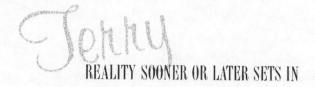

REALITY SOONER OR LATER SETS IN

I sat down and carefully planned out my weekend. Everything had to be perfect. I wanted to make sure everything was airtight. Angie wasn't like any of those other chicks I dealt with; not to mention I hardly saw her. If it didn't make sense to her, she was going to ask questions. I couldn't have anything fucking the night up. She had class, cash, and an ass that just, *MADE ME WANNA HOLLA!*

I picked up the phone and called Ty (my little cousin Tyrelle) so he would know the drill. Couldn't have him not knowing what was going on. Knowing my wife, she'd probably call him first looking for me.

"Hello," he said, answering the phone.

"What's up, Ty?"

"Shit! Trying to find something to get into tonight," he replied.

"Why don't you just call up Jodi or something?" I asked.

"I would if I could 'cause I damn sure need some ass right about now, but she's in Chicago. I'll fuck around and probably call April or something. I'll explode waiting for Jodi's ass. I need some now! What's on your agenda for tonight?"

"Tonight? It's more like the weekend."

"Nigga, you do remember Tracy? You know, your wife? Sometimes I think you forget that you're a married man. How in the hell are you going to spend the whole weekend with a bitch?" he questioned.

"Don't question me. I know how to handle myself and this situation, thank you very much. That's actually why I'm calling you. If Tracy calls you tomorrow, just say that I'm with you. Say I'm asleep or something. She won't try to wake me. I doubt she'll even call, but just in case. Can't have two different stories."

"So who's the lucky lady getting all this special treatment?"

"You'll never guess. I meant to tell you the other day when I ran into her. Man..."

"Who?" Ty asked, cutting me off.

"Angie."

"Damn! For real? I haven't heard that name in a minute. Slim was tough though."

"Was? You should see her now. She's off the hook! I tell you! When they say certain things get better with age, they ain't lying!"

"So, what has she been up to?" he asked.

"Hell if I know. We weren't talking about any of that. I was just trying to set up a time to get back in that."

"Yeah, I know *you* were. I bet your ass was happy to see that some things haven't changed."

"Who are you telling? I thought she would be like naw, 'cause of how shit went down the last time, but she was game for everything. I'm talking 'bout she was telling a brotha how she misses me and shit," I said.

"So, how are you going to pull all this shit off? If I remember correctly, slim doesn't know your ass is married, so I'm sure she's going to want you to stay with her the entire weekend," he said.

"Did your ass forget who taught you what you know?"

"Here we go with this again. You taught me a lil' something," he said.

"I taught your ass more than that, so I'm pretty sure I can handle this situation."

"Okay, how?" he asked.

"First of all, Tracy isn't going to miss me. She'll probably be out with her girls or something. She does her own thing on the weekends now."

"That might be true, but I'm sure she'll recognize that her husband didn't come home that night and that's when the shit will hit the fan. Y'all may be going through this lil' beef phase now, but not coming home will put ya on a whole other level. I'm taking the Divorce Court level."

"I'm sure it would, but who said I wasn't coming home tonight?"

"What? Did you tell Angie already that you're not spending the night?" he asked.

"No, I told you I didn't tell her anything. I just set up the weekend festivities."

"Then how are you going to get out of it, 'cause you know she is going to want your ass to spend the night?" he asked.

"Look, it's simple. Usually I get home from the club around what? 3:30-4:00 a.m.? So, I'll make sure I'm home Friday and Saturday night around that time. I did tell Angie that I'm having a house built out in Fort Washington and it's not ready yet, so I'm staying with you," I explained.

"Okay, that takes care of her spending the night with you, but not you with her," he replied.

Good point! Then what do I do? I was stuck.

"Damn, good question. I didn't think about that. I see what you're saying. That just stops her from staying with me, but she'll still try to get me to stay with her. I can say I don't have any clothes or something like that? Naw, that sounds childish. If I don't stay and don't have a good excuse, she's going to question the shit out of me. I go through that enough with Tracy. I'll be damn if I'm going to put up with it from someone else."

"How 'bout this? I'll just call you on your cell round 3:00 a.m. to give you an excuse to roll. Tell her that something came up and we need you at the club. That should take care of Friday night," he said.

"What if she asks what happened?"

"Tell her I didn't tell you. All I said is we need you at the club ASAP. She'll probably still be pissed, but she'll have a good enough excuse not to trip. That way it won't fuck up any ass for you on Saturday night. As for Saturday night, I don't know how you're going to get out of that, but if you can't come up with anything, just roll. She didn't trip off the cruddy shit you did last time, so she'll eventually get over it if you roll Saturday night, too."

I liked it. His plan was perfect. I'd still be home around my usual time so Tracy wouldn't expect anything. On Saturday, I could just carry it like Ty said and just roll. It wasn't like I'd be seeing Angie anytime soon after that. Plus, I wouldn't have to hear her bitch.

"Sounds like a plan to me," I replied.

"Why didn't you call me earlier this morning or something? If you'd given me more time, I'm sure I could've thought of something, other than you just carrying her."

"Naw, don't trip. I like it. I mean, I'm not trying to carry her, but I would've already gotten the pussy, so why trip if she's beefing? She leaves Sunday morning and I won't have to hear that shit."

"Just make sure you call Jeff and let him know what's up, too. Tracy might surprise you and call him instead, then you'll really be up shit's creek," he said.

"I will. You just make sure you remind him again at the club later on tonight as well. You know how his memory is."

"You don't have to tell me. You know I know. He has fucked up many an excuse for me on several occasions. I still think it's a miracle that Jodi and I are back together in the first place."

"Hold up now; that wasn't his fault. I don't know why you keep putting that on him. I would've done the same thing if I was him. You didn't tell anybody shit. How was he supposed to know that you had that chick at your house?" I asked.

"How was I supposed to know that Jodi would pop up over the house? She hadn't said anything when she'd called earlier that day about it and she didn't leave any messages saying that she would either. I thought I'd be straight since she'd called and I didn't answer. She had to know that I wasn't home. That was supposed to give me the time to fuck Slim and get her up and out of there."

"Your first mistake was giving Jodi a key. If she has a key, she has access to surprise your ass whenever she feels like it. Your second one, your dumb ass took another chick to your house. You know better than that! You do your dirt at her house or at a mo mo," I said.

"I didn't know she was coming over," he repeated.

"Bottom line, that shit was stupid. Deep down inside you know your ass was wrong. You can't even fake! You know you can't blame Jeff. All you had to do was let us know what was up and we would've made sure she didn't come over, regardless of who she'd called."

"I don't blame him for saying that he didn't know where I was. It was when he told her, '*He should be in the house. His ass is probably sleep and doesn't want to answer the phone.*' Now that was just stupid. That basically gave her the idea to come over," he said.

I could see his point.

"I see what you're saying, but what you don't see is that you usually tell us when you have something popping off. You didn't tell us anything that day. So how was he supposed to know? When your ass is sleep you don't answer the phone for shit. We all know this, so I could see why he said that. It sounded like the truth. Honestly speaking, Jodi usually leaves you alone when you're asleep. That time, she didn't. I mean, come on, Ty. Do you really think he would've told her that shit, if he'd known you had a bitch over?"

"I know he wouldn't but, still, he should've just left it at he didn't know where I was and then called me and told me she was looking for me. I mean, what if I was over Shortie's house instead? Jodi would've still come over and seen I wasn't home. Now I'm getting the shit questioned out of me when I walk through the door. And what if I'd fuck up by saying I was over Jeff's house. I would've been caught right there, and let's not forget I would've been walking up in the house smelling like pussy."

Even though he was dead wrong to blame Jeff for that situation, he'd found a way to make his point and it was valid. Even if that would've happened, he still would've been short.

"That's my point! If you have something popping off you should tell one of us in case she does call. Don't leave us in the dark 'cause I'll be damned if I'm calling you every time Jodi calls looking for you and I don't know where you are. What do I look like?"

"Whatever. I wasn't wrong. I don't care what you say."

"Weren't you the one who just told me to call Jeff and let him know the deal in case Tracy calls him?"

"That's different."

It was pointless. He was going to have his point of view and I was going to have mine. I just needed to agree to disagree.

"I'm not even going to keep going there with you. I don't feel like you can blame him. I know one thing, I bet next time your ass won't bring a chick over your house. I'll tell you that much!"

"I bet I won't either," he replied, laughing.

I heard the front door close.

"Lemme holla at you later. Tracy just walked in."

He agreed and we both hung up.

I grabbed my clothes for the night. I needed to hurry up and get out of there before she found a way to start an argument. The only way I could prevent them was by staying gone as much as possible. I'd make the dinner arrangements when I get to the club.

I went into the bathroom and turned on the shower. It would've been nice if she was asleep by the time I got out. I took a quick shower to freshen up. I walked out of the bathroom with my towel on and saw Tracy lying on the bed relaxing, watching TV.

"Where are you going this early?" she asked.

"I'm going to work."

"Can you take off tonight?" she asked.

I should've known. Every time I have something planned with another chick she wants us to do something. It's like she has ESP or something.

"Not tonight, baby. Maybe another time."

She moved over towards me and took my towel off. She began to massage my dick, teasing me.

"Come on, baby. I'm tired of all the arguing between us. I want to spend some time with you. I'll make it worth your while."

She began to give me oral pleasure that was better than usual. I couldn't believe what was going on. What had come over her? I pushed her off me. I was determined to have my night with Angie.

"Stop! Stop! I have to get out of here. Another time, baby."

"It's always another damn time when it comes to me! I'm getting sick of this shit. I had to play second to basketball in high school and college. Thank God your ass didn't make it in the pros, or we'd probably be divorced by now."

She realized what she'd just said. I remained calm.

She continued, "I'm sorry. I know how you feel about that situation. I didn't mean it like that. We hardly do anything anymore but argue. I don't care if we go to a movie or the mall; just take me somewhere. I don't care if you try to fuck me in a parking lot; just show me, in some kind of way, you're still attracted to me. Buy me an ice cream cone. I just want to spend some time with you because at the rate we're going, this marriage isn't going to last that much longer."

I had to pick and choose my words to avoid an argument, but anything short of me agreeing would've started one regardless.

"I know, baby, and I agree, but I can't tonight. It's the first of the month and I have to do the books and so forth. That's why I'm going in early. Why don't you call up Crystal tonight and do something with her and we'll spend next weekend together? I promise."

I grabbed my clothes and began to put them on. She gave me a look of frustration.

"Fine. Maybe Crystal can give me some dick," she said to aggravate me.

She got up and went downstairs. I felt bad for turning her down. It had been a while since we'd done something together. She was actually reaching out to me and I didn't grab on. But how could I? Who knew when the next opportunity to hook up with Angie would happen? I couldn't pass the chance up. I continued getting dressed.

I walked downstairs and saw Tracy sitting on the couch, watching TV in the living room.

"Baby, I promise we'll do something next weekend; just me and you."

She just nodded her head as if to say, "Whatever."

ALSO AVAILABLE FROM
STREBOR BOOKS INTERNATIONAL
All titles are in stores now, unless otherwise noted.

Baptiste, Michael
Cracked Dreams 1-59309-035-8

Bernard, D.V.
The Last Dream Before Dawn
0-9711953-2-3
God in the Image of Woman
1-59309-019-6

Brown, Laurinda D.
Fire & Brimstone 1-59309-015-3
UnderCover 1-59309-030-7

Cheekes, Shonda
Another Man's Wife 1-59309-008-0
Blackgentlemen.com 0-9711953-8-2
In the Midst of it All (May 2005)
1-59309-038-2

Cooper, William Fredrick
Six Days in January 1-59309-017-X
Sistergirls.com 1-59309-004-8

Crockett, Mark
Turkeystuffer 0-9711953-3-1

Daniels, J and Bacon, Shonell
Luvalwayz: The Opposite Sex and
Relationships 0-9711953-1-5
Draw Me With Your Love
1-59309-000-5

Darden, J. Marie
Enemy Fields 1-59309-023-4

De Leon, Michelle
Missed Conceptions 1-59309-010-2
Love to the Third 1-59309-016-1
Once Upon a Family Tree
1-59309-028-5

Faye, Cheryl
Be Careful What You Wish For
(January 2005) 1-59309-034-X

Halima, Shelley
Azucar Moreno 1-59309-032-3

Handfield, Laurel
My Diet Starts Tomorrow
1-59309-005-6
Mirror Mirror 1-59309-014-5

Hayes, Lee
Passion Marks 1-59309-006-4

Hobbs, Allison
Pandora's Box 1-59309-011-0
Insatiable 1-59309-031-5

Johnson, Keith Lee
Sugar & Spice 1-59309-013-7
Pretenses 1-59309-018-8
Fate's Redemption (May 2005)
1-59309-018-8

Johnson, Rique
Love & Justice 1-59309-002-1
Whispers from a Troubled Heart
1-59309-020-X
Every Woman's Man 1-59309-036-6
Sistergirls.com 1-59309-004-8

Lee, Darrien
All That and a Bag of Chips
0-9711953-0-7
Been There, Done That
1-59309-001-3
What Goes Around Comes Around
1-59309-024-2

Luckett, Jonathan
Jasminium 1-59309-007-2
How Ya Livin' 1-59309-025-0

McKinney, Tina Brooks
All That Drama 1-59309-033-1

Quartay, Nane
Feenin 0-9711953-7-4
The Badness (May 2005)
1-59309-037-4

Rivers, V. Anthony
Daughter by Spirit 0-9674601-4-X
Everybody Got Issues 1-59309-003-X
Sistergirls.com 1-59309-004-8

Roberts, J. Deotis
*Roots of a Black Future: Family
and Church* 0-9674601-6-6
Christian Beliefs 0-9674601-5-8

Stephens, Sylvester
Our Time Has Come 1-59309-026-9

Turley II, Harold L.
Love's Game 1-59309-029-3

Valentine, Michelle
Nyagra's Falls 0-9711953-4-X

White, A.J.
Ballad of a Ghetto Poet
1-59309-009-9

White, Franklin
Money for Good 1-59309-012-9
Potentially Yours 1-59309-027-7

Zane (Editor)
Breaking the Cycle 1-59309-021-8
(March 2005)